SAVING SARAH

The Gold Coast Retrievers, Book 1

MELISSA STORM

Sweet Promise

SWEET PROMISE PRESS
PO BOX 72
BRIGHTON, MI 48116

To Polo.

The Golden Oldie who stole my heart and inspired this series.

Free Gift

Thank you for picking up your copy of *Saving Sarah*. I so hope you love it! As a thank you, I'd like to offer you a free gift. That's right—I've written a short story that's available exclusively to my newsletter subscribers. You'll receive the free story by e-mail as soon as you sign up at www.MelStorm.com/Gift. I hope you'll enjoy both stories. Happy reading!

Melissa S.

Chapter One

SARAH LET GO of her patient's hand and watched as it settled back on the rumpled hospital blanket. Just yesterday Mr. Hinkley had regaled her with stories of his youthful heroics, of his time spent serving their country in Korea, and of the big, loving family that came after.

For more than eighty years he'd lived life as best as he could figure out how… and now?

He'd died alone in a nursing home, attended only by a nurse and her faithful therapy dog.

Her Golden Retriever whined and nudged the old man's hand one final time before looking to Sarah for guidance.

"Good job, Lucky," she whispered to the dog while pulling herself slowly to her feet. Sometimes she cried when residents left them. Other days she just felt numb. Whatever the particular case, saying that final goodbye never got any easier.

Not for Sarah, and certainly not for Lucky.

"Let's go for a walk," she told the dog as they click-clacked down the hall.

Lucky wagged his tail weakly. They both needed the warm California sun on their faces to coax the life back into them. It was part of their routine— treat, comfort, move on. If they mourned too long, then they wouldn't be on their best game for the other patients who needed them.

And so many needed them.

Each new person who passed through this facility offered Sarah a new life to try on, a new person to become. Outside of her work, her life had been rather unremarkable. She'd always done what was expected when it was expected. She'd gone to school, received straight A's, stayed out of trouble, and treated others with as much kindness as she could muster. Sarah was a good person, but not the kind anyone would remember when she herself passed.

She'd been working at the Redwood Cove Rest Home for the past four years now, and more than three of them with Lucky at her side. Of course,

Sarah hadn't originally planned to turn her pet into a colleague, but now she couldn't imagine herself getting through the day without the big yellow fur ball with her every step of the way.

When she'd first approached Carol Graves about adopting one of her famous Golden Retriever puppies, Sarah had only wanted a companion. Once she had secured a degree, a job, and a home, adding a dog to the mix seemed the natural next step. And because Sarah always did her best in all things, she naturally chose the most respected breeder in the entire state.

Carol Graves only bred one litter per year—and only Golden Retrievers. She'd devoted her life to the breed when one such dog had saved her from drowning as a little girl decades before Sarah had even been born.

Most of Carol's dogs went on to work in service, rescue, or even entertainment. In fact, when Sarah had first met the wriggling litter of two-month-old pups, she'd been immediately drawn to a frisky little female who was later named Star. Star now served as a co-host for the local cable morning show. Both Sarah and Lucky enjoyed watching her each day as they ate their breakfast.

But while Sarah had been drawn to Star, Lucky

only had eyes for Sarah. Of course, the erstwhile breeder insisted the two were meant to belong to each other—and that was that. Lucky actually came with his name, too. Carol had named him on the day after he was born. She hadn't expected the tiny runt of the litter to survive the night, but he'd surprised her and earned his name in the process.

Lucky had grown into a big, strong adult. No one would ever have guessed he nearly died the same day he was born. Maybe it was that near brush that made him so good with the hospice patients now. He'd been where they were going. He understood and wanted to help.

Which he did. Sometimes Sarah felt as if Lucky was the real medical wonder and that she was merely his assistant.

The Golden Retriever had a knack for knowing which residents were nearing the end, and he made sure they were never without cuddles in their final days. Once they passed on, he switched his attention to Sarah, who felt each loss deeply, no matter how hard she tried to toughen up.

Each death meant losing a patient, a friend, and a life she had tried on while enjoying all the stories and memories—temporarily adopting them as her own.

It was easier that way. Easier than finding her own life and making sure she lived it perfectly.

Just as the breeder Carol Graves had chosen her profession to celebrate a life saved, Sarah Campbell became a hospice nurse to honor the life she'd failed to rescue.

It had been her job to keep her grandmother company that summer day, to help her with anything she needed, and to keep her safe. Sarah had only been fourteen then—far more interested in talking with the attractive twin guys next door than in hearing another of her grandma's rambling stories for the millionth time.

Sarah's selfishness had meant she wasn't there when her grandmother needed help remembering whether she had taken her medication or not. In search of her wayward granddaughter, she'd slipped out of the house and down the front stairs. The ice-slicked steps led to a terrible fall she was just too weak to recover from.

Sarah still remembered the scream. It hadn't been loud and earth-shattering like you'd imagine, but rather meek—a tiny bird letting out a small, shaky chirp as it fell from its nest and crashed to the ground below.

That was the end of one life for Sarah and the

start of many others. Yet no matter how many she helped in their final days, she could never quite find a way to forgive herself for letting her grandmother down, for killing the old woman she'd love with her negligence. Even moving clear across the country, to a place where the winter months remained bright and sunny, hadn't alleviated her guilt. The only relief she had was in doing her best, giving her full attention to those who were left.

Just as she and Lucky had done for poor Mr. Hinkley. They'd done everything by the book. And still... still, she couldn't shake the enormous feeling of disappointment.

As she passed through the automatic doors and headed outside into the facility gardens, Sarah wondered if she would ever have great stories of her own to tell, if her life would ever become more than a vehicle for her heavy guilt, if a change was coming... and if she would welcome it when it arrived.

FINCH JAMESON HAD NOTHING LEFT—NO family, no job prospects, and not too much money, either.

Had it really only been five years since he'd been named one of the top thirty business tycoons under thirty?

Yes—five *long* years.

He'd made that list exactly one time before he bought into his own hype and ruined everything. Now, instead of being among the top thirty brightest young minds in the country, he'd become the number one failure, the poster boy for wasted potential.

Growing up, all he had wanted was to take beautiful pictures with his endless parade of yellow disposable cameras. He'd once aspired to be a nature photographer—to see his name in big bold letters plastered across *National Geographic* magazine. Once he hit his teen years, his passion shifted to fashion photography and all the gorgeous models such a career path would bring trotting through his bedroom.

Then, in his second year of college, a stroke of genius took hold of him and refused to let go. With a huge vision and an even more massive team of helpers, Finch brought his big idea to life.

Reel Life.

His fledgling social media network quickly overtook the flashing gifs of MySpace to become the go-to place for people to share their lives with the world. Reel Life Finch watched as MySpace Tom sold big and went on to enjoy a relatively anonymous and carefree life.

And he wanted that for himself.

He'd had his time in the spotlight and was ready to travel the world, taking pictures and enjoying every single moment of every day.

He eagerly agreed to sell Reel Life to the first person who asked.

As it turned out, he sold far too soon and for far too little. Seemingly overnight he went from "the one to watch" to the laughingstock of the free world. Luckily, neither of his parents had lived long enough to see his fall from grace. Still, Finch could have benefited from their love and support at the time when all the rest of his friends—and girlfriends —had abandoned him.

With nothing left, he abandoned LA to settle in the small coastal town of Redwood Cove. The money went fast, mostly due to a string of poor investments and bad advice.

"Why don't you just come up with another idea?" everyone asked.

But Finch was fresh out of brilliant inventions. Reel Life had been the pinnacle, and now at thirty-one years old, his life was already on the decline. His blazing passion for photography dulled to the tiniest of sparks buried within a giant mountain of dying embers.

It was all just too painful, too much of a reminder of what he'd not only lost but willingly given away.

Somewhere in the midst of yet another day whittling away at the time between waking up and going back to sleep, a letter arrived.

Not an email, but an old-fashion letter scrawled carefully in large looping cursive.

Dear Finch, it read, *I'm your great aunt Eleanor, and I'm dying. There's something very important I need to tell you before I go. Please come see me at the Redwood Cove Rest Home. I pray this letter finds you well… and before it's too late to set things right.*

Regards,
Eleanor Barton

Finch read the letter three times over before

folding it back up and slipping it into the torn envelope. A great aunt? No, that was impossible. His mother loved celebrating what little family they had. She wouldn't have let them grow estranged from one of the few surviving relatives.

He'd never once heard of the Bartons. Why would this sickly old woman reach out to him? How could she have gotten her wires so badly crossed? Made such a huge mistake?

He had half a mind to crumple the letter and toss it in the trash. This clearly wasn't his problem. But then again…

His imagination conjured a withered old waif of a woman staring forlornly out the window waiting for her lost nephew to return to her side. Could he really let her die thinking her attempt to mend fences had been met with cold refusal?

He didn't owe this woman anything, but he also couldn't live with yet another burden on his conscience. It was bad enough he'd tossed his own life in the crapper. The least he could do is help this sweet old lady find her family.

One good deed for the day, then he could return to his lackluster life.

Chapter Two

SARAH AND LUCKY arrived at their favorite local bakery about twenty minutes later. The day just needed something sweet to get itself back on track.

"Hi, Lucky boy! Hi, Sarah!" the shop owner, Grace, shouted cheerfully from her place behind the counter. She wore an apron patterned with tiny smiling blue whales on top of a deep purple background. It brought out the green flecks in her eyes. Sarah had always been envious of Grace's obvious happiness. It shone through in everything she did, from ringing up purchases at the cash register to gossiping about the latest town news.

Sarah liked Grace but never accepted any of the woman's attempts to make plans to see each other outside of Sweets and Treats. Grace's constant cheerfulness made Sarah weary. Was there really so much to smile about each and every day?

Sarah forced a smile of her own. "Hi," she said, swallowing down the beginnings of fresh tears. "I'll have two of your big cinnamons—make one sugar-free—a cheese Danish, and a pistachio pup cake for Lucky, please."

The corners of Grace's mouth pinched into a delicate bow. "Uh-oh. I know that order. You lost another resident today."

Sarah nodded. "Mr. Hinkley. In a better place now, thank God." She never knew what to say in these situations. One would think she experienced them enough to know exactly how to talk about death, but no. All she had were the same simple platitudes as everyone else.

"I'm sorry for your loss," Grace said. "Order's on me, of course."

"You don't have to do—"

"I insist." Grace reached forward and squeezed Sarah's hand, giving her a long, lingering gaze. *It's okay to talk to me,* she seemed to be saying. *It's okay to be vulnerable, to let others in.*

But Sarah preferred to spend days like this in her own head rather than rehashing details with others. Of course she was sad. Of course none of this was easy. How would it help admitting that aloud?

Instead, she remained silent and watched as Grace packed her order in the bakery's signature pink boxes. The giant donuts would make the rest of the staff feel better, as well as the residents who were closest to Mr. Hinkley. Each donut served six people, a local oddity that was every bit as delicious as it was unusual.

"It will be a few minutes on the sugar-free," Grace called out apologetically as she headed into the back kitchen. "I have to make that one fresh."

Sarah nodded and pulled her phone from her pocket, browsing with one hand and holding Lucky's leash loosely with the other. Apparently, she had three new notifications on Reel Life.

When she clicked on the app, a video of tiny wriggling newborn pups nursing on their mother, Rita, greeted her. Peyton McIntyre and Felicity Stilton had already commented along with dozens of others who had adopted puppies from Carol Graves.

"Look, Lucky," Sarah said, lowering the phone so the dog could see. "You have a new batch of brothers and sisters."

Lucky smiled and winked, which probably had

more to do with the gourmet dog treats behind the glass display case than with the birth of a new sibling litter.

She needed to leave a comment or Carol would worry about her. Even all these years later, she still made sure they all stayed in touch and that she got pictures of each of her grand-dogs at least once per week.

Sarah snapped a picture of Lucky in front of the bakery case and posted it as a reaction to the video. "Lucky is celebrating with his favorite treat! Congrats on the new litter!" She then added three heart emojis and snuck the phone back into her pocket.

"Here we go," Grace said as she bustled over to the front counter. "Be careful, it's extremely hot."

"I'm always careful," Sarah said with a nervous laugh. Grace, of course, had no idea how true that sentiment rang for most things in Sarah's life. Burning her mouth on a hot pastry was the least of her worries these days.

Although Sarah lived a small and safe life, she was never short on anxiety. She knew they couldn't go on forever like this—Lucky and her. Eventually, things would change.

Sarah would decide she wanted more, or her mother would decide for her. It was only a matter of time before all the deaths added up, became too much to bear, and then what would Sarah do with her life? Then whose memories could she hide inside?

One day at a time, she reminded herself as the warm breeze lifted her hair from her shoulders. She and Lucky trotted quickly down the sidewalk and back toward work.

First, they needed to get through today. That's all they had to do, and then everything would be okay.

FINCH'S HEART refused to quiet. It pounded a steady beat in time with his footfalls as a nursing home aid led him down the long white hall toward the woman who believed herself to be his great aunt.

Was this all some big misunderstanding? Or was it possible that he actually did have a family after all? He didn't know what to hope for in this scenario. If Eleanor Barton truly was his long-lost aunt, then he'd only have a family for a short while until her illness overtook her and he was alone in the world once more.

Having no idea what to expect, Finch hadn't prepared himself for the visit at all. Perhaps that was why the smell caught him so off guard—first the stinging sensation of bleach as he sucked the lingering chemicals through his nostrils, then something musty stuck to his insides long after the cleaning solution smell faded away.

Death, Finch realized. *This is what death smells like.*

"She's right in here," his guide said with a smile, stepping aside to let Finch pass through. "Mrs. Barton," the orderly called, keeping his feet rooted to the hallway floor. "Your grandson is here."

"Nephew," Finch corrected gently. "Maybe."

"I'm not a missus, and he's not my grandson," the old woman corrected far less gently.

The orderly forced another smile; this one remained tight at the edges as if to keep certain choice words from escaping. "Well, I'll just let you two get reacquainted then. Buh-bye now."

Neither spoke until the echo of shoes slapping linoleum faded in the distance. Finch kept his eyes on the floor, but he could feel Eleanor studying him closely.

"I got your letter," he said at last.

"About time," the old woman said with a huff. Although she had to be at least eighty years old, her skin was still mostly smooth. Did that mean she'd lived a lifetime without feeling? No smiles, scowls, or anything else to mar her complexion? What kind of life must that have been? And was Finch already on his way to upkeeping this apparent family tradition?

No, he couldn't get ahead of himself. Not until he knew for sure. Not until he had proof.

He cleared his throat before asking, "I don't understand. If you're really my great aunt, then how come I never knew you existed before?"

She shrugged as if he'd asked a simple question instead of an impossible one. "You'd have to ask your parents that."

"I can't. They died," he whispered, feeling their loss all over again.

"Well, I suppose that's for the best."

"How could you say that? Did you even know my parents?"

Eleanor directed her attention toward the large window that overlooked a courtyard below. Her face remained impassive. "Hardly," she answered after an unnaturally long pause. "But it wasn't through any fault of my own."

Finch's eyes widened as he waited for her to tell him more.

She didn't.

"Are you really my aunt?" he asked on the wings of a slow, tortured exhale.

"Are you really Finch Jameson?" she shot back with a lightly raised brow and a knowing glance.

"Yeah. That's me." How much did she know? Had she lured him out for his money? Was she intentionally toying with him? And just how much was he willing to put up with before he stormed out of there and never looked back?

Eleanor straightened in her chair and locked her eyes onto his. "Then yes, I'm your great aunt. You have her eyes, you know. The same ocean blue."

"You mean my grandma? Nancy?" he asked hopefully. The doubts he'd brought with him to this meeting slowly ebbed away.

"Yes, they're one in the same. Anyway, Finch…" She paused and took a long breath. "I can't say I'm surprised at how you turned out, but I also can't say I'm all too pleased, either."

Well, that took a sharp turn. Perhaps no family was better than a hostile one. Maybe he *should* leave. "Hey, just a second… You don't even know me."

"Don't I? I know enough to understand that you're a disgrace, a failure. That people laugh at you behind your back—and probably to your face, too." For all the strength her body lacked, Eleanor's tongue clearly made up for it.

Finch crossed his arms and tore his eyes away from his frail bully. "But not enough to know my parents died years ago? Look, if you called me here just to mock me, then no thank you."

Eleanor clucked out a sound midway between a sarcastic laugh and a growl. He recognized it as the same derisive snort he'd often heard his own mother make. "You flatter yourself," she said. "You're not here for you. You're here for me. Now sit down and listen to what I need to say."

"Sorry, no. Family doesn't mean much to me, seeing as I haven't had any for years." He raised his voice before dropping back to a stern whisper. "I'm just fine without it, too."

"So that's it? I point out one universally understood truth, and you run away? No wonder you failed at business... probably failing at life, too, I'd imagine."

"Well, at least I have one left to live," Finch hissed, turning back toward the door, hoping to high heavens he'd never see Eleanor Barton again.

But he was stopped by an angel—an angel and her dog.

"Is everything okay here?" the woman asked. Her long blonde hair fell over her shoulders in soft California waves. Her round face was offset by bright hazel eyes and a cute, upturned nose. And her smile... her smile did funny things to Finch's heart, which suddenly seized in his chest as if it needed to slow down to remember this moment.

Wait.

Don't go yet.

Maybe I...

Maybe he needed to give this long-lost family member a second chance at a first impression... especially if it meant getting to spend more time in this angelic woman's presence.

"Everything is great," he answered at last. "Nurse...?"

"Sarah," she said simply. "Call me *Sarah*."

Chapter Three

SARAH HAD BEEN SURPRISED to find the orderly peeping into Ms. Barton's room. Most of the staff avoided the cantankerous Eleanor, especially when she was having one of her off days. What was more surprising, though, was finding a good-looking stranger storming out from that very same room.

"Is everything okay?" she squeaked, nervous to be speaking with such an attractive member of the opposite sex. Sarah and love didn't mix, had never mixed—it was why she preferred to spend all her free time with her dog instead.

"Everything is great," he answered breathlessly, making Sarah wonder if he, too, had felt a spark upon meeting. But, of course, that thought was ridiculous. Men never noticed Sarah. At least not any younger than seventy years old.

"Nurse...?" He let his words fall away as he awaited an introduction.

"Sarah," she told him, brushing her palm against his.

"I'm Finch. Finch Jameson." he said, squeezing her hand for longer than was customary for a simple greeting.

"Is Ms. Barton your...?"

"Pain in the backside?" he asked with a laugh. "Yeah, it would seem so. We just met for the first time, but according to her, we're related."

"But you're nothing like her," Sarah argued, comparing the brassy senior lady with delicate features to this sandy-haired, ocean-eyed man before her.

He shrugged, but she could tell something was bothering him. He wore the evidence in the furrow of his brow, in the rapid pace of his pulse.

"Well, are you coming or going? I haven't got all day, you know!" Eleanor called from within the room.

"Yeah, I've noticed," Finch confided in Sarah with a sigh.

Sarah decided to take a chance. Funny she

thought of it as a chance when really she was just doing her job. But instead of filling out paperwork about Mr. Hinkley's passing, she asked the handsome visitor, "Would you like me to stay with you? To help make you... her... more comfortable with talking?"

"I'd love that." A smile lit up his entire face, making Sarah doubt even more that he bore any relation to Ms. Barton.

Sarah shook her head and breezed into the room. At least she hoped she breezed, seeing as her feet felt like they had a one-hundred-pound weights tied to them. "C'mon, Lucky," she called cheerily. "Let's see how Eleanor is today!"

The dog pranced across the linoleum and placed his muzzle in the old woman's lap.

She appeared to tense for a moment before slowly beginning to run her fingers through his soft fur. Everyone loved Lucky—it was impossible not to.

She caught Finch watching her, waiting for her to break the ice in this odd situation. Sarah put on her work voice and a smile. "So this is the nephew you told me about. Is it?"

"How'd you know?" Finch asked, crossing his arms and leaning against the far wall. He seemed afraid to come too close, as if his aunt were an untamed lion rather than a sickly old woman.

"I helped her mail the letter. Besides, we have our chats every morning. Your aunt's lived a very interesting life."

Of all the lives Sarah tried on, she always had the most difficult time wearing Eleanor Barton's. Here was a woman who had never been married, never gone to college, never had any children of her own, yet somehow still managed to find fault with everyone's life but her own. Would Sarah wind up like her one day—old, alone, and ornery?

She blushed when a vision of her and Finch standing at the aisle flashed before her eyes. *Oh, if only!*

"Don't patronize me, dear," Eleanor grumbled, though her face held the promise of a smile. "You and I both know my life has been unremarkable. I've kept it that way on purpose."

"Because you were scared?" Sarah asked, identifying with the resident more than she cared to admit even to herself.

"Do I seem like a shrinking violet to you? No, not scared. Just protecting those I loved most in the world. But now that they're dead and I'm going that way soon, there's nobody left to protect. Seems it's time for the truth to come out at last."

"What do you mean?" Finch asked, uncrossing his arms and drawing closer. "Do you have some kind of terrible secret?"

Eleanor waved a hand dismissively. "Don't be so melodramatic. It's not a good trait for a man to have."

"Eleanor," Sarah interrupted, "what truth needs to come out? Why did you reach out to Finch? How can he—*can we*—help?"

Sarah gulped down the lump that had begun to form in her throat and waited. Perhaps Eleanor Barton's life wasn't as dreary as she'd led everyone to believe. Perhaps she'd prove them all wrong in the end, leaving a glistening legacy behind when she went.

Perhaps...

But there was only one person who could tell them for sure.

And she seemed to have lost her voice.

FINCH LEANED BACK against the wall, too agitated to sit while they all waited for Eleanor to spit out her big revelation. "Well?" he prompted when the old woman still hadn't begun her story.

She sighed and brushed out the wrinkled clothing on her lap. "There's really no easy way to say this," she spoke at last, fixing her eyes on the dog instead of either Finch or Sarah. "I called you here as my nephew, but you're not really a part of my family. Not by blood."

Sarah inhaled a sharp breath and called Lucky to her side with a quick flick of the wrist. "I thought you reached out to him because he was the only family you had left," she said steadily. Each word came out clear and without judgment.

Finch, on the other hand, had lost his patience long ago. First, they were family, then they weren't. What was the truth, and why had she called him here?

Eleanor sighed as if it were them who were agitating her. "Well, yes and no. We are family... of a sort."

He couldn't believe this, didn't want to believe it. He hesitated briefly before asking, "Was I adopted?"

"Not you, your grandmother."

"She was adopted," he repeated with disbelief.

Why had he never heard any of this before? And why should he believe it was true now?

Eleanor shook her head subtly. Her mouth formed an *O* around the word before it even slipped out. "*Stolen.*"

"I should go," Sarah said, inching back toward the door. "This is obviously a private matter."

Finch grabbed her wrist before she could fully make her escape. "Don't," he said as a tiny spark shot from his fingertips and zoomed straight toward his heart. "I think we both need you here. That is, if you don't mind staying."

Sarah sent a worried glance toward her patient, who nodded encouragingly. "Okay," she said meekly before sinking into a chair at the edge of the room. The whole time Lucky remained glued to her side, eager to help in whatever way he could.

"My grandmother was stolen. You *stole* her?" he prompted, hoping Eleanor would finally explain in a way he could understand.

"Not me personally. My sister. I'd say, 'God rest her soul,' but there's a very good chance she's in the other place after what she did."

"What did she do?" Sarah asked, her eyes glistening with curiosity or perhaps the beginnings of tears.

"It's really quite simple, now that you know the gist of it," Eleanor answered dismissively. "She and her husband wanted a baby but couldn't have one. The war had just ended, and it seemed like everyone else was having babies faster than you could say 'welcome home, soldier.' They didn't have the technology back then, so it was really quite easy for her to walk into the hospital by herself and walk out with a new daughter to call her own."

Finch's arms dropped to his side, the life kicked right out of him as the full force of Eleanor's confession hit him in the gut. "My grandma?"

The old woman nodded and looked away again. "Your grandma."

"How come nobody ever said anything before? Did my grandmother know? Did my mom know before…?"

"Your grandmother found out around the time she was eighteen. She never said another word after that—to any of us. As far as I know, she never spoke of the incident again."

The rage returned with fresh strength. Who or what gave this woman the right to break apart his family back then to bring it all to his doorstep now? The worst part was he knew deep down that it was true, the doubt already swept clean away.

"*The incident?* That's what you're calling it? You kidnapped her, stole her from her rightful family, her rightful life."

Eleanor turned red beneath his blistering gaze. "Again, I didn't have to tell you anything. I could have taken my secret to the grave, you know."

"Then why didn't you? Why drop this bomb on me when there's nothing I can do about it? Do you know who my grandma's real parents were?"

She shook her head, then pointed up at him. "No, but you're going to find out."

"*Me?*" He narrowed his eyes at her. This was no family he wanted in his life, no secret he wanted to help uncover. "What makes you think I have any desire to help you?"

"I don't know you, and you don't know me, but I took a gamble that you'd be too curious to just walk away. It's your legacy, after all." She looked to Sarah and Lucky for encouragement, but both stared ahead with slightly ajar mouths.

Finch shook his head, wishing he could turn back time, throw that letter from Eleanor away the moment it had arrived. "Why do you care? Why does this even matter if all the original players are already dead?"

Her voice dropped to a murmur. "Because the

kidnapping was just the start of it. Other things happened after. *Bad things.*"

She looked so frail then, suddenly beaten down by the burden of the truth she'd been carrying on her own until that day. Still, Finch couldn't forgive her for the trouble she'd caused his family then and was causing him now.

"Bad things is pretty vague," he pointed out. "What happened? What am I walking into by agreeing to help you?"

Eleanor's hands shook on top of her lap. Her breaths came out in labored puffs as she struggled with whatever it was she still needed to say.

Sarah rushed to her side and spoke soothingly in her ear.

Finch couldn't make out the words, but when Sarah returned to her seat Eleanor seemed stronger, calmer.

"So you agree?" Sarah asked, straightening in her chair and watching as Lucky licked Eleanor's hands and face. "You're going to help Eleanor set things right?"

"Grant an old woman her dying wish?" Eleanor added with a sarcastic chuckle.

Finch hesitated. This was all way more than he had asked for. He still didn't even know if the old woman had spoken the truth. His logical brain questioned every last detail—although there were precious few he'd been granted—but something deeper knew. Had always known.

"I want in, too," Sarah said, startling him with the ferocity in her voice. "I'm going to help however I can. That is, if you'll let me."

Chapter Four

SARAH TREMBLED as Finch's eyes met hers. She hadn't given it much—or really *any*—thought before volunteering to help Finch find his true family and to put Eleanor's guilt to rest. Her inner critic screamed in protest.

What am I doing? I don't know the first thing about any of this! He probably doesn't even want me around. It's all in my head.

Finch took a step closer. "Why would you want to help me?"

She swallowed, tried to force a confidence she didn't feel into her voice. It was too late to take her offer back now. "Not you. *Eleanor.* It's obviously important if she went through all this effort to find you."

Finch rolled his eyes and laughed bitterly. "I'm not really hard to find, though. Am I?"

Bile rose from Sarah's stomach, but she swallowed it back down. Why had Finch's attitude changed so significantly? One second he'd begged her to stay, and the next he seemed angry. She stared at him blankly, waiting for him to explain what she'd missed.

But he just shook his head and sighed. "Don't you know who I am?" he asked with wide blue eyes as if there were some answer other than *dreamy stranger, man she would dream about for days if not months to come.*

"And I was worried I'd make it awkward," Eleanor joked from her seat across the room. Sarah's awkwardness seemed to put her at ease. Oh joy!

Lucky licked Sarah's hand, then rubbed his nose between her slack arm and her hip so that she'd be forced to pet him. Forced to relax.

"You introduced yourself as Finch Jameson. I mean, the name sounds familiar, but I just figured it was because Finch was a trendy name these days." She shrugged, having not thought anything of his familiar name or appearance before. But now she wondered whether their paths had in fact crossed before. Then again, how could she forget such a handsome face, such a kind—well, *normally* kind—smile?

"You don't know me?" he asked in disbelief, his expression softening.

"I don't know you," she parroted with emphasis on each word.

"So you just want to help to be… what? Nice?" He laughed sarcastically, causing Sarah to question everything. How could she have misread the situation so entirely? Finch Jameson wasn't a kind man, and he didn't want her help.

She turned toward the door, running over every possible excuse in her head. Was it too late to get away?

"Oh, stop," Eleanor interjected. "Not everyone has an ulterior motive these days. Nurse Campbell is a genuinely nice person. She puts up with my crap better than anyone else here, and you'd be *lucky* to have her at your side."

At the mention of his name, Lucky sat and waited for a command.

"Okay," Sarah said to the dog, releasing him from his hold. "Thank you, Eleanor," she whispered to the old woman, who sat waiting with an expectant look on her face. It was the first time

Sarah had ever heard her say anything nice about anyone. Normally Ms. Barton was quite conservative when it came to admitting she liked or enjoyed anything.

Punishment for a guilty conscience, perhaps?

"I could use the help," Finch admitted at last. His smile finally returned. "Seeing as I have no idea where to get started."

Sarah looked away as an intense new heat rose to the apples of her cheeks.

"I'm sorry about before. I'm not used to people being, well, *real* with me." He laughed, though Sarah failed to understand whatever joke he'd made.

"One condition," she said, eliciting a pair of bemused expressions from her companions. If she was really going to do this, to spend time with this man who was both handsome and confusing, then she needed her life line.

"Now there are conditions?" Finch asked with raised eyebrows.

"Just one: where I go, Lucky goes."

Lucky perked up at the second mention of his name and trotted to Sarah's side.

Finch frowned. "I'm not sure he—"

"That's non-negotiable for me. I really want to

help you both, but I need Lucky at my side in order to do that."

"He agrees," Eleanor answered for Finch.

"Okay, fine." Finch let out a long, slow breath. A slight smile flashed across his face only to be replaced by a sudden look of consternation. "So you, me, and Scooby are going to solve a mystery, but where do we even start?"

Eleanor grabbed her cane and used it to pull her hunched form into a standing position. "That's the easy part. You start at the beginning."

Finch stared blankly ahead, waiting for an explanation.

Sarah had understood perfectly, though. "We need to go to the hospital where she was born," she whispered.

FINCH WATCHED as Eleanor hobbled across the room with no obvious destination in mind. "Where are you going?" he asked as Sarah rushed to offer aid to the old woman.

"Isn't that obvious?" Eleanor asked between soft grunts. "I've said what I needed to say, and now I'm going away."

Lucky whined, his dark eyes shifting anxiously between the three people in search of answers.

Well, Finch didn't have answers, and he felt like whining, too. "But you haven't told us anything," he said, chasing after Eleanor, which wasn't hard to do given her intensely slow speed.

She sighed. "You know *enough*. Enough to get started, anyway."

"No, I don't. Tell me, where is the hospital?" Finch placed a hand on her shoulder, startling them both in the process.

Eleanor paused for a moment, thoughtful, before murmuring over her shoulder, "*Fine*. I'll tell you this piece and that will be the end of this conversation. It's the big one in San Francisco."

Finch tried to be thankful for this one piece of information, but it was hard to be relieved when there was so much more that Eleanor wasn't saying. He hoped his voice didn't come across as irritated as he felt. "Well, that's one thing out of a hundred we still need to know."

Sarah drew close and put a hand on her forearm. "Just let her go for now," she whispered.

But Finch was not to be deterred. Now that he'd been dragged into this, he needed to know what had really happened with his grandmother and what it would mean for him now.

A thought suddenly occurred to him. "When was my grandmother really born? Did she ever know her true birthday?"

Eleanor made no attempt to hide her annoyance. "If the answers were easy," she hissed, "I would have told you by now. I've said what I can. The rest is up to you."

"What? *No.* Is it because of the bad stuff you mentioned?"

Eleanor simply shook her head and kept walking.

"If it's so bad, why didn't you fix any of this earlier? Why leave it to me? Why say anything at all?"

Still no response.

"Hey, you can't just walk away. I need answers!" he shouted as the old woman turned into the long corridor. Perhaps they were related after all. They both had a stubborn streak a mile wide and matching tempers, too.

The same orderly who'd originally led him to the room appeared and took Sarah's place at Eleanor's side.

"She needs rest now," Sarah said with downcast

eyes. "We need to respect that."

"But did you not hear what I just heard? At the very best, this woman is a liar and at worst, a criminal. How can you just let her run away?"

"Run?" Sarah chuckled. "She's hardly moving at a stroll, let alone a run. She says she gave us enough to get started, and I believe her."

"How? How do you know any of this is true?"

Sarah looked pensive. "I don't, not really. But I choose to believe her."

"Why?"

"If we find out she's lying, then we'll have gone on a wild goose chase with all of this, maybe lose a few hours of our day. But if she's telling the truth and we don't believe her, then what? She'll die never having closure, and you'll never find your lost family." Sarah clicked her tongue and Lucky trotted over to her side, placing his rump on the floor and his head between her hand and hip.

"I still don't get why you want to help with this."

"Honestly, it will be fun. Don't you think?"

Finch cleared his throat before answering with, "None of this is fun."

"Because you're still in shock. It will wear off. Trust me." She bent down and gave Lucky a kiss on his forehead. The dog lapped up her every attention.

"It sounds like you've done this before."

"Maybe," she said with a sad smile, leaving Finch to wonder what ghosts now floated across her mind, how many patients she had helped and then lost.

Finch forced a chuckle. Somehow they needed to clear the air here, make things less awkward between them. "Are you sure she's not just senile?"

"That's rather ageist of you," Sarah answered with a small frown. "Why does everyone always assume the elderly are already half gone, that they've lost their minds? Actually, they know so much more than all the rest of us, have experienced so much more. It's a terrible thing to say, especially about your own aunt."

Well, that didn't work. Finch needed to defend himself but wasn't really sure how. He began to argue anyway. "But—"

Sarah cut him off with a laugh of her own. "Relax, I'm just giving you a hard time. But it is a pet peeve of mine. Look, you can live the rest of your life assuming everyone is lying or crazy, that everyone is out to get you, or you can choose to have faith in them. I will always choose to believe. It makes for a far less miserable life."

Sarah's choice of words didn't escape him. How could such a sweet-seeming woman be so discontented with her life? "Less miserable? As opposed to happy?"

"Yeah." She twisted her fingers in Lucky's fur, refusing to meet his eyes.

Neither said anything as they stood together in the bleached-out hallway.

He had three choices then. He could walk away from all of this, he could go after Eleanor, or he could take his chances with Sarah. He chose the only option that had any silver lining at all. Time with a beautiful, kind woman wouldn't be so bad— no matter what they found. *Right?*

"Okay," Finch said at last. "I choose to believe, too. Whether or not any of this is true, I still don't know. But I'm ready to go find out."

Sarah shook her head and chuckled. "It doesn't sound like you believe yet, but I'm glad you're willing to try."

"What do we do next? Can I take you to dinner?"

Sarah chewed her lower lip for a few seconds

before answering with an emphatic *no*. "Not dinner. I'd have to keep Lucky at home, and part of our agreement was that where I go, he goes. So how about the dog park? At five? We can make our plans there."

Winning Sarah over would not be easy. Maybe it wouldn't even be possible, but Finch wanted to try. He reached out his hand to shake on the deal. "Okay, the dog park it is then."

"Thanks, I'll meet you there." Sarah brushed a strand of hair behind her ear, then clicked her tongue and took off down the hall with Lucky trailing at her side.

Oh, what a day this had turned out to be.

And it wasn't even close to over yet…

Chapter Five

SARAH FELT Finch's eyes on her as she marched down the familiar halls. Even after she'd found cover in a waiting patient's room, she felt him with her. What was she thinking not only volunteering to help but *begging*?

While it was true the prospect of a mystery to unravel excited her, it was also true that she couldn't deny her attraction to the man who'd been assigned to help her solve it. Nothing about this was good. Falling in love had never been in the cards for Sarah, and she'd also never been a one-night-stand kind of girl. So where did that leave her and Finch?

Heart-deep in frustration, no doubt.

But it would only be for a short while. Sarah's forays into others' lives never lasted long. How could they when she spent nearly all her time with folks already at death's doorstep?

Finch, on the other hand, was very much alive —strong, vibrant, and with a bit of an attitude problem. Sarah could handle attitude and often did with her patients, but while it was easy to rebuff the advances of the old men who said she reminded them of their loves from long ago, what would she do if Finch put the moves on her?

Probably run screaming into the night.

I'm only doing this to help Eleanor, she told herself over and over again, hoping she could eventually convince herself it was true. It was on the three-hundred-and-something repetition of this new mantra that she finally found something else to focus on.

"I was your age not so long ago," a new patient named Agatha told her in a trembling voice as Sarah checked her vitals. "I was pretty like you, too, with a natural curl to my hair. Made me very stylish back then."

"I bet you were a great beauty in your day," Sarah answered with a smile. She knew better than to point out that the woman was still beautiful, just in a different way. When patients wanted to journey to the past, they didn't need anyone pulling them back into the harsh reality of the present. That's part of the reason why she lived out their glory days alongside them. It was like falling in love, finding an adventure, and following your dreams again and again.

"Of course," Agatha continued, "by the time I was your age, I already had two little ones with a third on the way. It was different back then than it is now."

Sarah couldn't stop herself from asking, "Tell me about your husband. How did you meet?"

Deep crow's feet formed around the corners of the old woman's eyes even before the smile reached her lips. After letting out a dreamy sigh, she said, "The same way everyone did in my day—at the local church. Albert and his family moved to my town after the war. I saw him that Sunday wearing his creased trousers and a shirt that was too large on his thin waist, and I knew he was the one I wanted to love forever."

"Forever?" Sarah said, her eyes widening. "You saw him and you knew it was love? Just like that?"

"Just like that," Agatha said, closing her eyes. Sarah wondered if she was picturing that first glimpse of her beloved now, if she was mourning the loss that had brought her here to live out the rest of that forever on her own.

When she opened her eyes again, she smiled at Sarah and said, "Love at first sight is very real. You'll know when you find the one that's meant for you."

Before Sarah could stop it, her mind conjured up an image of Finch saying hello, saying goodbye, asking to see her again. His tranquil blue eyes, the sharp cut of his jaw, the sandy tones in his hair... There was no doubt she found him attractive.

But to love?

Nothing so magical had happened as it did for Agatha and Albert.

So she had a crush on one of her residents' relatives. It had happened before. It would happen again. There was nothing special about Finch Jameson, just as there was nothing special about Sarah Campbell. They were simply two people whose paths had crossed, who were meant to come together for a short while and then continue on their journeys alone.

I'm just doing this to help Eleanor, she reminded herself yet again.

"I'm going to let you get some rest, Agatha," she said, motioning to Lucky to take her place at the old woman's side. "But I'll leave Lucky with you for a bit of extra company while I finish my rounds. See you in the morning."

She gave Lucky the hand signal that meant *stay* and left Agatha's bedside in search of Eleanor. She found her a short while later in the community room watching a hummingbird at one of the many feeders while wearing a blank expression.

"Eleanor?" Sarah said softly, coming up beside her.

Eleanor hummed a beat in acknowledgment but kept her eyes glued to the planters outside. Sarah wondered if she even saw the beautiful flowers, butterflies, and birds before her—or if her mind was far off somewhere else.

"About today…" Sarah hesitated, not wanting to rile the old woman's temper. "Is there more you can tell us so Finch and I know where to start?"

Eleanor frowned, a rare expression of true emotion on her stoic face. "You already know where to start, but perhaps this will help." Reaching into her cardigan pocket, she pulled out a folded sheet of lined paper torn haphazardly from a spiral notebook.

Sarah reached out for the paper, but Eleanor kept it close to her chest.

"First I want a promise from you. No matter what you do or don't find, please make sure he doesn't hate me in the end."

"Of course not. How could he hate you?" Sarah patted her arm, wishing she'd brought Lucky with her. He was better at comforting the patients than she'd ever been.

I'm only doing this to help Eleanor, she repeated. This time, it was easier to believe.

"Just promise me and know that I've already suffered more than my share these years. I'd hate to lose the only bit of family I have left in the end. Especially since I'm trying to set things right before I go."

Sarah nodded. "I understand, and I promise."

"Then this is for you." Eleanor pushed the paper into Sarah's hand and then turned to leave the common area.

Sarah waited until she had gone, then carefully, reverently, unfolded the paper and read the list of words and numbers scrawled in cursive across the page:

Lotte,   *13055270433894134,*   *Bear,*

2407530012415494132,   *Karda,*

1112554598794134,   *May,*
1103563307924188,   *Editor,*
290257129312493942, Green.

It went on and on and on. First a random word, then a big string of numbers. Again and again…

None of it made any sense.

None of it helped at all.

FINCH HEADED BACK HOME and prayed the hours would pass quickly. The innkeeper, Joshua, greeted him warmly. His service dog sat alert beside him.

"Have a good day?" Joshua asked from his usual place in the main lounge area.

"Yeah, I guess you could say that," Finch answered as loudly as he could without yelling. He didn't feel like getting into it, especially with Joshua, who had lost most of his hearing during combat and wasn't exactly the easiest choice of conversational partner.

Still, he was a good guy.

In another life, he and Finch could have been

great friends. However, in this one, seeing Joshua always reminded Finch that the other man's life had changed because of a heroic sacrifice and Finch's had changed due to sheer stupidity and poor planning. It always made him feel guilty envying the disabled veteran as he did. He probably didn't have deranged great aunts insisting a mystery be solved before time ran out. But he also didn't know Sarah, the beautiful angel of a nurse who had come to his rescue today who Finch would be seeing later tonight…

Or did he?

Finch eyed the service dog again. His name was Charlie and he always stood at Joshua's side, nudging his hand or tugging on his shirt to act as his owner's ears. Was it possible that Lucky and Charlie might be related and thus the owners might somehow know each other?

He shook his head as he let himself into his room. Even if they did know each other, what did it matter? Sarah was interested in Eleanor's mystery, not in Finch. And he couldn't blame her for that. No one was interested in Finch anymore unless they needed a good laugh at his misery.

Sarah was different in the best of ways.

Perhaps her lack of awareness regarding his

very public embarrassment is what endeared him to her, but he also felt as if something more was there—just beneath the surface waiting to be discovered.

———————

THE HOURS PASSED SLOWLY, but at last the evening came and to the dog park Finch went. In his eagerness to see Sarah again he arrived a bit too early. Actually, twenty-two minutes early.

Groaning at himself, he took up a seat on an old wooden bench in the shade and watched strangers' dogs run in and out of the surf in pursuit of balls, sticks, and other projectile objects. Their owners stood in a huddle, chattering with each other and throwing the odd toy whenever one of the dogs brought something back.

Do they do this every day? Finch wondered.

Would getting a dog add some stability to his life, allow him to meet new people, people who didn't care about his failures in the business world but rather about how his day had been, or which trick his dog had learned?

Maybe.

At least it was something to think about once all

this business with Eleanor Barton had been brought to a satisfactory close.

That's all he did now. He got by one day at a time.

Once a long time ago, he'd had passion, true excitement for the future. Back then it had been his love for nature, plants, animals… the big wide wild as he'd called it then. As a little boy, he'd begged his parents for a dog, but they'd only ever conceded for a cat—a devil of a Maine Coon named Mr. Kerfluffle. Finch didn't much care for the cranky feline but he loved taking pictures of him basking in the sun, lapping up water from his dish. Sometimes he'd even let Mr. Kerfluffle outside against his mother's orders so that he could photograph him among the flowers in the garden.

He smiled at the memory and pulled his phone out of his pocket. He rarely carried a camera with him these days, the joy of his once fervent passion having largely been extinguished when… well, you know.

Everyone knew. Except, it seemed, for Sarah.

Alone with his thoughts and the anticipation of seeing sweet Sarah once more, Finch felt the beginnings of a spark. It would be short-lived, he knew, but still, he just had to capture a few photos while he waited. There was something magical about the way the water splashed up around the short legs of a Basset Hound as he charged into the tide.

Finch zoomed in and snapped several pictures of the hound before moving on to a large mixed breed who would perfectly resemble a Pitbull if not for his long, wiry hair. He was an odd and intriguing fellow who shook off a hurricane of tiny droplets each time he exited the water.

He sat reviewing his photos and chuckling to himself when a yellow blur shot across his peripheral vision and Sarah appeared at his side.

"Hey, those are pretty good!" she said, glancing at his phone over his shoulder. "Could you take some of Lucky, too? I'd love to have a few decent shots to post on Reel Life."

Finch sighed and jammed his phone back in his pocket without first nabbing a couple shots of the happy Golden Retriever. He studied Sarah briefly, trying to remember the way she looked at him when he was just somebody's long lost nephew and not a national disgrace. "You really don't know who I am, do you?"

As expected, her features crumpled in confusion, apprehension. "I told you I don't."

"And you didn't Google me?" There was no

avoiding it. If he didn't tell her, someone else would… and likely soon.

"Why would I? Besides, we just got off work and came straight here." Sarah plopped herself down onto the bench at his side and held out her hand with a smile. "Now, if I give you my number, will you take some pictures of Lucky and text them to me please?"

Finch handed her his phone so she could input her number and text herself his contact details. Once she'd finished, he took a deep breath and began.

"Sarah, listen. I think there's something you should know about me…"

Chapter Six

SARAH SAT QUIETLY as Finch explained who he was and why she should know about it. Apparently he was this big social media icon like Mark Zuckerberg—only with far better looks but also far less business savvy.

"So you made a mistake," she said when he'd finished his tirade. "Big deal. And, to be perfectly honest, I never much cared for Reel Life anyway. It doesn't really seem like you did, either."

Finch began to tap his foot in agitation as he leaned back on the bench "What's that supposed to mean?"

"*It means* you started it because you love taking photos, but it turned into this huge thing that you no longer felt you had any control over. Maybe getting out *wasn't* a mistake. Maybe it's what your heart wanted, and it's just your brain that's having a hard time understanding." Sarah leaned back, too, so she could study his reaction as she spoke. His insecurities helped to dispel her own, giving her a rare burst of confidence.

Finch stared at her in dumbfounded silence, but the rigidity in his form softened. Her words seemed to provide at least some measure of comfort for his past hurts. Was it Finch's head or his heart that found peace with Sarah? Both, she hoped.

She continued, emboldened by the slight smile that had briefly flashed across Finch's face. "And you know what? It feels like social media has become this huge obligation, something most of us have to do but don't really want to. If you ask me, it's all a big waste of time." She grabbed her phone out of her purse and brought up the home screen.

"What are you doing?" Finch asked, leaning forward, leaning in close.

Sarah tried not to let it distract her. She had a mission to complete. "Deleting my account and then getting rid of this app."

"What? You don't have to—"

She jerked her phone away so he couldn't try to take it for safekeeping. "I want to, Finch. We have a mystery to solve, and the last thing either of us needs is all these pings and notifications distracting me and upsetting you. Right?"

"I guess so," he mumbled.

Sarah clicked through a surprising long sequence of screens to confirm deleting her account. Once she'd finally reached the last one, she waved her phone triumphantly in front of Finch.

"That felt really good," she admitted. Of course, she'd be in for it when the breeder Carol Graves found out, but Sarah could deal with that later.

After shoving her phone back into her purse, she withdrew the note Eleanor had given to her earlier that day. "Take a look at this," she said, handing it to Finch. "Does this mean anything to you?" They sat hip-to-hip, each studying the string of words and numbers on the paper, their only clues toward finding Finch's lost family.

He shook his head sadly. "I don't get it. It's mostly numbers. Dates, maybe? But dates for what? And what do the words mean? *Bear? Editor?*"

"I was hoping you'd know because I sure don't. But, look, there are a few names, too." She drew her finger to *Lotte, Joseph, Julie*—each written in

Eleanor's shaky hand. "I figured we could start with them."

"You didn't Google me, but you're going to Google them, huh?"

"No, you are. You seem to be much more tech savvy than me anyway."

"Okay, and then what? Because I'm not sure how far I can get with just first names here. Or if we're even reading them right. This writing is—"

"But we at least have to try, right?" Sarah felt her heart quicken as she was overcome by the very real worry that they would never get anywhere in solving this mystery. She'd made a promise to Eleanor, and she couldn't stand to disappoint her, to fail at delivering her final wish in life.

"Of course we're going to try," Finch said, briefly touching Sarah's hand and sending her heart galloping for much nicer reasons.

Sarah felt the heat rise to her cheeks, speaking quickly to get them past this moment, get them back on track. "I traded shifts with one of the girls at work for tomorrow so that we can make a trip over to the hospital. Pick me up at seven and we'll head out to see what we can find."

"So are we heading in without a plan?" Finch shot a photo of the list, then handed the paper back to Sarah for safekeeping. Their fingers brushed again. Was it intentional on Finch's part this time? Was he also daydreaming about what it would be like to hold her, to kiss her?

She gulped hard, praying that Finch couldn't read her thoughts, that tomorrow would be easier. "Yeah, pretty much, unless you're able to find something during your fun-filled night of Googling."

"No pressure or anything," he said with a laugh.

"Not a bit." She gestured to his phone before he could shove it back into his pocket. "Now that that's decided, can you take some actual pictures of Lucky for me? I've never had him professionally photographed before, and I'd love something nice to hang on my wall."

"Okay, c'mon." He stood and offered Sarah his hand so that he could also pull her to her feet. "I'll give you a few pointers while we're at it. Soon you won't need me at all."

Not need Finch? Oh, Sarah very much doubted that. Already she found herself terrified of what would happen once they solved their mystery and went back to not having a valid excuse to spend time in each other's company.

Either they would find a way to be together… or they wouldn't.

And honestly, she didn't know which was worse.

FINCH STAYED at the dog park long after Sarah and Lucky went home. He liked it here, liked that he once again felt like he belonged to something bigger than himself.

Something real.

Maybe all he'd needed was a bit less hiding in his room and a bit more time spent in the open air. Would he wake up in the morning to find things were different now? Would the shame at least be erased, and might the future finally hold hope for something good?

He could almost let himself believe. Sarah had urged him to believe the best of others, and he wanted to. But could he extend that own courtesy to himself?

He spent hours locked in quiet contemplation. Every time new hope swelled within his heart, a sharp and stinging memory came to deflate it. He'd see Sarah's delicate features, blonde hair, and pink cheeks and feel the first whispers of happiness. But then he'd remember the articles, the interviews, the market reports, and his joy would plummet faster than a falling stock.

Back and forth his mind zipped until, at last, night fell and the fireflies began to flash their tiny lights all around him. No more of this. It was time to head home and put this bizarre day to rest. Only time would tell if it had been the beginning of something wonderful or a new kind of nightmare to contend with.

A long-lost aunt, an intriguing mystery, an entire evening at the dog park sans a dog of his own, and quite possibly a new love interest, too.

But why would Sarah want him?

Sweet Sarah, who saw the best in everyone whether or not they presented it. Sarah who loved dogs and saved lives on a daily basis. Sarah who was just as humble as she was beautiful. Sarah who'd deleted her Reel Life account to show her support for a man she'd only just met.

He brought out his phone as he walked back to his car and typed her name into Google. After all, she was the one who'd ordered him to spend the evening poking and prodding the search engine.

Thousands of results popped up. A Sarah Campbell smiling for a family portrait. A Sarah Campbell kissing her boyfriend on the cheek. A

Sarah Campbell eating brunch at some ritzy city cafe.

None of them were *his* Sarah Campbell, though.

Narrowing by location didn't help. He simply couldn't find the needle he wanted in this giant haystack…

So what made him think he had any chance of solving Eleanor Barton's big mystery of more than seventy years in the making? This wasn't even a wild goose chase. It was more like wandering around in the darkness without a flashlight.

But then he thought of Sarah, how her whole face lighted with a pink glow whenever she spoke about his mystery—*their* mystery. For reasons he didn't understand, she wanted to be a part of this. And if he gave up on Eleanor, then it would also mean giving up any chance he might one day have with Sarah.

No matter how much his brain screamed at him to leave this foolishness aside, his heart insisted that he see where this could go.

The mystery.

The romance.

The possibility of having a family once more.

That night he made no progress decoding the

list, but it wasn't the mystery he wanted to crack. He'd much rather figure out a way to break through Sarah's remaining walls. Occasionally, she offered him a glimpse of what lay on the other side and—oh—how he longed to be there with her.

Still a few nagging questions remained.

Why did she need Lucky in order to see him? Did she want him the way he thought he might want her? Was she afraid of her own feelings or, like Eleanor, might she have a terrible secret lurking behind that sweet, sweet smile?

That was when he realized he was far more interested in unravelling the mystery of Sarah Campbell than in helping the cruel, old Eleanor Barton.

And, well, if he had to help one in order to help himself to the other…

Then that's exactly what he would do.

Chapter Seven

SARAH PULLED her hair into a messy bun at the nape of her neck, studied her reflection in the mirror, and then let her mass of frizz fall loose again. She paced back to her closet and looked at the mess of clothes inside, letting out a huge sigh as she crossed from one end of her apartment to the other.

Lucky whined and nudged Sarah's hand until she was forced to stop panicking long enough to pet him.

"Thanks, boy. I needed that," she said with a small smile. She felt calmer now, but no clearer on just what she should wear or how she should look for her day out with Finch. What *was* the proper attire for solving a seventy-year-old mystery with a wildly attractive failed billionaire? Polka dots? Plaid? A freaking ball gown?

She really had no idea, but if she didn't figure it out soon, she'd be wearing a bath towel when Finch came to collect her that morning. And that would definitely *not* be the right call.

Lucky winked at her, then spun in two circles before laying down on his doggie bed, leaving Sarah to decide on her own.

If she put in too much effort, he'd think she was into him. If she put in too little, he'd think she didn't have any feelings for him at all. So which was the right way to go?

Oh, this is frustrating!

At last she settled on her classic standby: jeans and a T-shirt with a high ponytail and only the slightest touch of makeup. It would have to do because she really couldn't waste another moment on this—and she shouldn't have wasted any moments to begin with. Finch was just a man, and Sarah already had all the male companionship she needed in her life thanks to one very attentive Golden Retriever.

"C'mon, Lucky," she called, closing the door to her bedroom behind them—mostly so that she would not be tempted to enter and change her outfit again. "Let's make breakfast."

She hardly had enough time to pour the fresh pot of coffee into two stainless steel travel mugs and grab a few pastries from the pantry before Finch showed up at her door.

Five minutes before the time they'd agreed upon. *Eep!*

"You're early," she said with a smirk, handing him a coffee mug and that stack of pastries as she breezed past him and toward his car.

He turned red beneath her gaze, and she loved knowing that he felt every bit as awkward as she did. It was as if only one of them could be weak at a time and the scales constantly shifted back and forth.

"Yeah, it's kind of a problem I have," he explained.

"Not a problem," she said as she pulled open the rear car door for Lucky and threw his favorite blanket over the back seat. "I think it's a good thing to have respect for other people's time. As long as you're not *too* too early, that is."

"Got it." Finch saluted as he dropped into the driver's seat and waited for Sarah to settle in on the passenger side. "So, are you ready to head to the City by the Bay?" he asked with gleaming eyes.

"City by the Bay, huh? Does that mean you're a local or a hipster? Maybe both?" Sarah had been in the Bay Area long enough to know that she shouldn't refer to the city as *San Fran* or *Frisco*, but she rarely heard it called anything other than its full name. Honestly, Redwood Cove already had everything she needed, which meant she rarely had cause to venture out of it.

"Definitely not a hipster," Finch said with a laugh she rather liked as he ran his hand across his smoothly shaven jaw. "But, yeah, Gold Coast born and bred. Not always in Redwood Cove, but I wanted somewhere a bit more private when…"

"When everyone with a blog and an audience was smearing your name?"

Finch surprised her with a smile. "So you Googled me at last."

"It seemed important to you," she mumbled, feeling her confidence sway yet again.

He shrugged before jabbing the keys in the ignition and bringing the engine to life. "I just want you to know who you're agreeing to spend your time with. What you're getting yourself into."

Sarah closed her eyes, preferring not to see the

expression on Finch's face when she told him what she really thought of his failed business venture. "Well, you seem pretty okay by me. Actually, you're kind of great, you know. You built an empire based on the strength of one idea. You went for it, and you weren't afraid to fail. I know I've never done anything like that."

"Yeah, well... I guess you know everything about me that's worth knowing now," he said as he reversed the car out of the parking spot and away from her apartment complex.

She hadn't expected him to pay her back with a compliment but still felt disappointed when one didn't come. Perhaps the fact that they were here together now was enough. "I doubt that," she said after a pause. "People are more than their Google search results, you know."

Finch scoffed. "Not anymore. Not in today's day and age."

"Now you sound like one of my patients," she said, rolling down the window and allowing her hand to ride on the breeze as they drove. "I like that."

"Have you always been super into old people?"

She stared at him for a second, then burst into laughter so fierce she couldn't even try to silence it.

"That came out wrong," he said, laughing, too. "You know what I meant to ask, so just answer *that* question, okay?"

She sobered up, sadness overtaking the effervescent laughter. "Not always, but since I was about twelve."

His voice softened as he cast a glance her way. "Why? What happened?"

"I… I don't want to talk about it."

Sensing her apprehension, Lucky whined and stuck his head over the center console so Sarah could stroke his fur. "It's okay, boy," she cooed.

Finch's voice became so quiet, Sarah had to strain to hear it over the whooshing wind outside. "Sorry, I didn't mean to get into anything too heavy. Obviously you don't have to share if you don't want to. Just trying to fill the time between here and the big city."

"You're fine," she said with a deep sigh. "Maybe someday I'll tell you, but not today if that's okay."

"Uh, yeah, of course." Finch frowned and drummed his fingers on the steering wheel. "Tell me something else then. Talk to me about Lucky."

"Now that I can do…"

Finch laughed in all the right places as Sarah described Carol Graves and her over-the-top commitment to staying in touch with every puppy that had ever been born from her kennel. He even threw in a few stories of his own about the cat he'd had while growing up. If discussing work and family was hard, then talking about their pets was like breathing in clean, sweet air.

If only it could always be this easy. If only she could one day love and trust a person the way she did her dog. Might today be a step in that direction?

Before she had time to contemplate the possibilities, Finch pulled into the sprawling hospital complex... and the easiness between them vanished into the endless summer sky.

FINCH TIGHTENED his grip on the steering wheel and let out a long, slow breath. They'd arrived, and yet he still had no idea what he really hoped to accomplish here.

"Are you ready?" Sarah asked, a waiting hand hovering over her seatbelt buckle.

Her dog Lucky panted excitedly in the back seat as all three of them took in the massive hospital complex before them. People died here, were born here, found out life-changing news, said final goodbyes, and maybe even learned long-hidden truths.

What would *their* visit bring?

He tried to push all these nagging thoughts aside and put on a reassuring smile, but Sarah saw right through him.

"Hey, it will be okay," she said, brushing her fingers against his forearm and igniting a spark that made the fine hairs stand on end.

Whatever happened next, he had Sarah at his side. It was funny how much that meant given they'd only met each other the day before. And while he craved the company of this new acquaintance, he feared what others might be brought into his life as a result of solving Eleanor's family mystery.

"Let's go," he said at last, swinging both legs out of the car before he could change his mind. He waited for Sarah to hook Lucky onto his leash, then the three of them marched toward the swinging glass doors.

Was it possible a whole new existence waited on the other side for Finch? Or would it only be more disappointment?

Predictably, nothing earth-shattering happened —only that they were greeted with scattered stares the moment they strode through those doors. Lucky wore his red harness identifying him as a therapy dog, so at least nobody gave them a hard time about bringing an animal into the hospital.

Finch paced to the greeting desk with far more confidence than he actually felt.

"How can I help you today?" a plump woman with short curls and a tired smile greeted him.

"I'm looking for information about my grand-mother," he said with a nervous smile.

The receptionist nodded and sat up straighter in her chair. "Oh, is she a patient here?"

"No, but she was born here in 1946."

"Oh, okay…" She hummed a beat, put on a fresh smile, and asked, "What information do you need?"

"Everything. Whatever you have." He startled when Sarah squeezed her shoulder.

"I'm not going far," she whispered, leaving him on his own at the front desk. He began to watch them clack away, but the perturbed receptionist broke his concentration almost immediately.

"Is this an estate issue?" she asked for what Finch assumed was at least the second time.

"No, I'm just trying to…" He let out a deep breath and sunk both hands into his pockets. He felt so vulnerable standing her alone, demanding secrets he didn't know how to put into words. "To learn about my family," he finished at last.

The woman's smile wavered as she began shuffling papers on her desk. "I'm afraid you'll have to put in a special request and provide proof that you're next of kin. We don't have digitized records that far back, so it won't be easy to find what you're looking for. And we just don't have the extra staff to—"

Finch raised a hand to cut her off. "It's fine. I get it. What about paperwork on my aunt? Eleanor Barton?"

This time she didn't even try to disguise her sigh before asking, "Is she a patient here?"

"No, but she would have been more recently."

"Okay…" She clicked a few keys on her computer, then handed Finch a print out. "You'll need the patient's written permission, proof of relationship, and-or power of attorney. Then we should be able to get those for you."

Finch rolled the papers into a tube and resisted the urge to give up and walk away. "Is there any way I can have any of these records *now*? We're kind of in a hurry."

"Not without the proper authorization. Hospitals have gotten in big trouble before for far smaller privacy violations." She spoke slowly as if it were the only way to make him understand. "I'm sorry, but there's really no way around the rules here."

"It's fine. Thank you." Finch let out a long, irritated sigh.

It wasn't the receptionist's fault, of course, but *still*. They only had one clue that made any sense, and it led to a dead end. Eleanor had been cagey about offering even the smallest of clues, so how would he ever get her to agree to sign the consent form?

And how would he get the needed proof to access his grandmother's records when it had been years since her death? Even if he got it, how long would it take for the hospital to find and deliver the files? And could he handle all that time knowing, but not knowing?

He turned back toward Sarah at a loss, hoping she would have the answers he was missing. But she and Lucky weren't standing where he'd left them. Instead, they had journeyed down the hall and were standing beside a small child wearing a hospital gown and sitting in a wheelchair.

Finch immediately noticed the short, patchy hair and the dark purple bruises beneath the child's eyes, but he couldn't tell whether the child was a boy or a girl—only that he or she was very, very sick.

Lucky sat, wagging his tail gently and allowing the child to press a hand between his eyes. The sharp squeal of a giggle that followed made Finch's heart break and melt at the same time.

"Lucky, *shake*," Sarah commanded, and obediently the dog offered the child its paw.

"His name is Lucky?" the child asked in a voice that now very clearly belonged to a girl and to one much older than he had expected —perhaps eight or nine instead of the five or six he'd assumed.

"Sure is. And what's yours?" Sarah said, crouching down so she was eye to eye with little girl in her wheelchair.

"Sara," the girl declared with a smile.

"Hey, that's my name, too!" Do you have an *H* at the end?"

The younger Sara shook her head and giggled. "Nope."

"See, *I* do," Sarah said with an infectious smile that Finch found himself loving more and more each time he saw it. "Which is good, because now nobody can get us confused."

Both Sarahs smiled at each other, and Finch could only watch in amazement.

Sarah Campbell didn't just have a calming effect on him—she had it for everyone. It wasn't in his head or imagined. She truly was the most amazing woman he'd ever met—and he felt himself falling for her faster than ever.

Chapter Eight

SARAH JUMPED when Finch put his hand at the small of her back. She'd been so caught up in speaking with the young girl in the wheelchair that she hadn't even noticed he'd finished at the registration desk.

Now that he was here, she felt herself relax into his presence. As awkward as things often were between them, she'd come to appreciate the way the air hummed melodically, the way her heart sped up before she'd even fully realized he'd returned.

Finch leaned in close to her ear and whispered, "I have an idea. Play along."

She nodded and gave little Sara a hug goodbye. "It was so nice to meet you, Sara without an *H*. Lucky, wave buh-bye."

The Golden Retriever did as instructed, eliciting giggles from both the patient and the nurse pushing her chair.

She smiled to herself at having made a new friend. As much as she enjoyed working with the elderly, there was something very special about sick children. The juxtaposition of innocent potential and the grave awareness of one's own mortality sent chills through her. Still, little Sara seemed so full of hope, as if death weren't even an option for her.

She said a silent prayer that this would prove to be true, that the sweet child would grow up to have and appreciate every experience life had to offer. Never mind that Sarah had chosen to forego many of the standard rites of passage herself.

"Bye, Sarah with an *H*!" the little girl called as she and her nurse continued their journey down the hallway.

Finch motioned for Sarah to join him back in front of the registration desk, and she did so without question. What kind of plan had he cooked up in the brief moments they'd been apart? She looked forward to discovering whatever his creative mind had concocted.

"Look," Finch told the woman sitting there. "I

know you couldn't help me, but we were hoping we could help you while I'm here."

The receptionist's eyes widened, but her mouth remained pressed in a flat line. "I'm not sure I follow, and the hospital definitely doesn't take bribes."

Finch laughed a bit too spiritedly for the situation. "You thought?" He shook his head as the chuckle faded away. "No, I'll be back about that later with the proper forms. But my friend here is a therapy dog."

He motioned to Lucky and suddenly Sarah understood. He needed a distraction. For what, she didn't know, nor did she really want to find out. Sarah played by the rules, plain and simple.

Finch, on the other hand, continued with gusto. "He usually works with the elderly, but he just loved meeting that little girl. Perhaps you saw?"

The receptionist smiled, for the first time looking genuinely happy to be in their company since they'd arrived. "It was very sweet," she agreed.

"Would it be okay for us to stop in for a quick hello at the children's ward? We did drive all this way, and we would love to put some smiles on faces while we're here." He regarded the comely woman with a smile, the same smile that made Sarah's heart twist and leap with nervous anticipation. No woman in her right mind could resist that smile.

And sure enough…

The receptionist hesitated, and a coquettish expression overtook her features. "I don't know. We don't have a therapy dog on the schedule for today, and besides, we've never worked with you before." She turned to Sarah with a much sharper, accusing tone. "How do we know you have the proper certifications?"

"Do me a favor," Sarah said, recognizing that the situation was headed in a very different direction than Finch wanted. "I'm a nurse at the Redwood Cove Rest Home. Lucky works with me there. Give them a call and they'll tell you what you need to know. We can wait while you check with the nurses on your ward, too."

Sarah took a step back and Finch followed suit.

"We'll just be in the waiting room. Whenever you're ready," Sarah informed them both.

Finch pumped his head in agreement. "We'd so love to see the kids. Wouldn't we, Lucky?"

Lucky thumped his tail and let out a soft bark, eliciting smiles from both the receptionist and Finch.

"What's your big plan?" she whispered to him once they'd taken a pair of seats at the far end of the waiting room.

His voice came out so quietly she had to strain to hear it. "I asked about my grandmother and Eleanor, but I can't get records for either without jumping through a bunch of hoops."

"Okay, so where do Lucky and I fit into this?" she asked, dread beginning to pool in her stomach.

Then his smile lit up again. This time its full force was directed squarely on Sarah. "Too much red tape. I'm going to see if I can find someone who has scissors."

She turned away from him and tried to think logically. Despite how much she wanted to solve this mystery, there was the right way to do things… and then, apparently, there was Finch's way.

He placed a hand on her arm, drawing her gaze back in. For a moment, she knew how Adam must have felt when Eve offered him the forbidden fruit. But it only took a second to find her center again. "No, Finch. This is wrong. You're going to get us thrown out of here."

"So what if I do? We're at a dead end anyway. Might as well see if we can turn this around. Besides, the kids will be so happy to see Lucky."

Well, now what could she say to that? She did want to help the children, but…

"I really don't know," she stalled, trying and failing to think up a more cogent argument. "There's gotta be another way."

That was when the receptionist appeared at the edge of the waiting room and motioned them all over. "We're ready for you now," she said without taking her eyes off Finch for a single second. "You can go on back."

So much for talking him out of it…

FINCH DIDN'T LOVE that he'd needed to resort to using the sick kids to pull one over on the hospital, but really… what else could he do? Sure, he'd call his attorney once they got back home, but would his corporate lawyer even know where to begin in order to get him the proper clearance? It's not like Finch had anyone in his family he could ask for help, either. The only family he had besides Eleanor was either dead or—apparently—missing.

He trailed behind Lucky and Sarah as a resident nurse led them to the children's wing. Despite the unplanned nature of the visit, the children and staff were both all too happy to meet Lucky. They soon learned that a Bichon Frise named Frankie visited the ward on most Fridays, meaning they already had protocols and procedures well in place for therapy dog visits.

With all the focus rightfully on Sarah and Lucky, Finch had no trouble slipping away. The problem came in deciding where to go and who to talk to. At first, he tried to find someone within the children's ward itself, but he quickly abandoned that idea, not wanting to embarrass Sarah—especially given her disapproval of his rule-bending plan.

Ultimately, he turned to the cafeteria, figuring an off-duty healthcare worker would be more amenable to his advances than someone rushing to tend to their patients.

Once there, he zipped through the food line and loaded various lunch items on his plate in order to appear as if he belonged, then wandered between the tables waiting for someone to cast an inviting look his way.

You can accomplish anything with a smile, his mother had taught him long ago. It was a lesson he never forgot, especially in moments of need.

And, sure enough, it didn't take long to find a kind-looking woman wearing scrubs that stood out bright and blue against her dark skin. When she glanced up from her meal tray, he saw that she, too, wore an arresting smile and had pointed it directly at Finch. She also appeared to be about his age.

"Mind if I join you, doctor?" he asked, holding his tray at waist height while awaiting her response.

"Sure thing." Her smile widened and she kicked out the chair across from her, motioning for Finch to join. "Thanks for not assuming I'm a nurse just because I'm a woman."

"You have a very doctor air about you," Finch said, biting into the sandwich he'd picked up without even noticing what kind it was. Egg salad, as it turned out. Not the worst thing in the world.

"I'm Nakeesha," she said between bites of a pear. "And you are?"

"Finch." He extended his hand and she accepted with a quick shake.

"Jameson, right? I thought you looked familiar. And I always thought the media was unfair to you."

"Thanks, I appreciate that." He smiled again. If not for his new infatuation with Sarah, Nakeesha would normally be the type of woman he'd ask for a date. It had been such a long time since he'd had a romantic encounter of any kind, and he couldn't imagine breaking his unlucky streak with anyone but Sarah Campbell, even if she didn't like his plan.

They ate in silence for a few moments while Finch worked up his nerve. This whole thing would be much easier if he could genuinely flirt with Nakeesha, but he'd just have to settle for being friendly instead.

"Listen, I was hoping you could help me out with something."

Nakeesha dropped her half-eaten pear back onto her tray and raised her eyebrows as if she already knew what he planned to ask. *How* he asked for this favor would be extremely important now.

"It's kind of strange, but I just found out that my grandma may have been switched at birth." Finch didn't like to lie but figured this version of his story would be better than explaining she'd actually been kidnapped due to hospital negligence. Nobody enjoyed having someone come into your workplace and tell you that you were bad at what you did. Finch had experienced enough of that on his own to know that he should avoid treating others to the torment and accusations he'd endured.

Nakeesha didn't seem shocked by his revelation. Her demeanor remained cool and collected. Was this something that happened more often than anyone wanted to assume?

"Oh, interesting," she said. "What makes you think that?"

"It's a very long story." He laughed, feeling encouraged when Nakeesha joined him.

He moved forward casually as if what he were about to ask for wasn't hugely illegal. "I need to review some records to be sure, but I'm getting nowhere with administration. Is there any way you could…?"

"Help you skirt the rules and access private records? *No way.*"

Uh-oh. He needed to save face and quick if there was to be any hope of securing Nakeesha's help. "I'm not trying to do anyone harm. I just have to know what really happened with my grandma. You understand, don't you?"

The young doctor shook her head. Her eyes grew wide, but she said nothing.

He spoke quickly now, desperately, stumbling over his words. "I can get the proper clearance, but I really don't want to wait if I don't have to. I'm sure you have a lot of student loan debt. I could help with that, if you help me with this."

Nakeesha pushed her chair back and jumped to

her feet. "*Unbelievable*," she shouted, encouraging those seated at nearby tables to scowl at Finch alongside her. "I never believed all the bad things they said about you, but maybe I should have. I know you had fun with your little website, but that wasn't real life. *This is.* And in real life there is no instant gratification, so go home and do the work. Also, might I suggest you not try this little stunt on anyone else before you go, or you'll never see those records—but you *could* see the inside of a jail cell."

Yikes! That had gone way worse than expected. Maybe Sarah had been right. Maybe he should have listened…

Finch fumbled his tray as he stood. "Nakeesha, wait, that came out wrong."

"Uh-huh. Sure, it did. I'm done here anyway, which means we're done."

He watched as she wove through the tables fueled by her anger toward him. So much for Plan B…

Chapter Nine

FIRST EMBARRASSMENT SPREAD into Sarah's limbs. Then anger.

She'd let this happen.

She could have stopped it, but that smile had instead stopped *her* from doing what she knew to be right. Of course, she was more than a little ticked when Finch admitted he'd tried to bribe a doctor into helping with their search.

"What else could we really do?" he responded to her indignation with a shrug, keeping his eyes focused on the road ahead.

"Oh, I don't know… Gone through the proper channels? Done exactly what the lady at the registration desk told you to do?" She let out a beleaguered sigh, for as angry as she felt at his total disregard for the rules, she also felt a little jealous. She'd never be so brave, so daring as to go after what she wanted like that. Which meant Sarah often didn't end up getting what she wanted in life. And that was why she'd stopped wanting more than she had. Better to be content on a small-scale than drowning in disappointment.

She swallowed her anger back down. Nothing truly bad had happened. At least not yet. Still, she wanted to understand, so she asked, "You've gone your whole life without knowing, what's the big rush now?"

"Making up for lost time?" Finch suggested with a boyish smile, again cutting any argument off at the quick.

"Well, you don't have to be stupid about it," Sarah said, crossing her arms over her chest to guard her heart. Every time she caught a glimpse of that smile, she felt her resolve fading. This Finch was dangerous in more ways than one.

He turned toward her then, his brows pinched together, his expression resigned. "You're right. I'm sorry."

"Good." Because she didn't think she could hold up her end of this argument much longer.

"Good." Finch's inquisitive eyes turned toward her. "So what next?"

"We can try talking with Eleanor again," she suggested, knowing even before the words had left her mouth that they held no hope for either of them.

He let out an exhausted laugh. "Cuz that got us really far the last time… What about the list?"

"What about it? We're missing the magic decoder ring needed to make any sense of it."

Finch chuckled, but Sarah did not. "Fine, I'll talk with Eleanor."

"No," Sarah said so quickly she startled the both of them. "*I* will. She likes me better than you, and besides, who got the list out of her, huh?"

"The useless list in code? *Uh-huh.*" The corners of his mouth began to rise in a grin, but Sarah whipped her gaze away before she could be caught in its disarming light.

"Whatever," she muttered and rolled down the back windows so Lucky could hang his head out and enjoy the rushing wind and so that she wouldn't have to attempt to speak with Finch over the noise. Anger bubbled up anew, but this time she didn't know whether it was meant for Finch, Eleanor, or for herself. Maybe it was just the impossible situation. After all, where could they really go from here?

There was only one way to find out…

"YOU WEREN'T HERE YESTERDAY," Eleanor Barton said when Sarah and Lucky breezed into her room for checks. "You were supposed to be here. I don't like the girl they sent in your place."

"Missed me, huh?" she asked with a surprised smile as she handed Eleanor her morning pills.

Eleanor shrugged and sat up taller in her bed.

"You don't have to admit it, because I can tell you did." Sarah waited for the old woman to swallow down her medicine and then added, "I was with your great-nephew yesterday, actually. We went to the hospital like you told us."

Eleanor grunted. "I can tell by the way you're looking at me with big puppy dog eyes that you still don't know anything."

She shook her head. "No, we didn't accomplish much of anything with our visit."

"Much of anything? Or nothing, because it sounds to me like you've got *bupkiss*."

Sarah took in a deep, centering breath. If her

attraction to Finch scared her, then her newfound fear of Eleanor terrified her. Still, they needed something to go on if there was to be any hope of solving this mystery. She smiled again, hoping her smile would have the same magic powers as Finch's. "I was hoping you'd be able to—"

"No." Eleanor Barton stared straight ahead, her face an uninterpretable mask.

Sarah searched for a way in—any crack, any way to reach this ornery old woman's sense of great good. "It would really help if—"

"*No.*" Eleanor turned on Sarah suddenly, but rather than adjusting her whole body, she simply whipped her neck in the other woman's direction. The movement was so sudden and came with such agitation that Sarah was reminded of the old *Exorcist* movies. Would Eleanor start spewing pea soup on her next?

Sarah forced herself to hold ground, which agitated the old woman even more.

"How many times do I have to say it?" she asked in a dry, low voice. "Don't you realize that it already took everything I had to tell you what you know so far? It wasn't easy, you know, seeking Finch out, making an admission like that. Can't you just leave me alone and do your job?"

Sarah reached to Lucky for strength. The dog sat still as she ran her fingers through the hair on his neck. Together, they were united—not against Eleanor, but against the needless hiding of the truth.

"I'm trying to help," she said, calmer now.

Eleanor snorted again. "Help yourself to my great-nephew, maybe. I know you've never much cared for me, so why else would you want to help?"

"But just the other day you said I was a genuinely nice person. Remember that?" From hesitation to fear to hurt. Just like her great-nephew, Eleanor Barton could make Sarah feel the full range of emotions in just a matter of minutes.

Eleanor turned away and mumbled, "Because I thought you'd be a help, not a distraction."

"I…" What else could Sarah say? Eleanor had made her mind up, and clearly there was no convincing her otherwise. "Okay, I'll leave you to yourself then. C'mon, Lucky."

"Leave the dog."

Rather than responding to Eleanor's demand, Sarah spoke directly to Lucky. "C'mon, boy. We have other patients to see."

No matter how much she tried not to let it bother her, Sarah's mind kept coming back to

Eleanor's accusation. Had Sarah really only wanted to help in order to spend time with Finch? If so, why was she still terrified of letting herself fall for him? And what would happen when the mystery came to a close?

FINCH'S DAYS moved by slowly after their visit to San Francisco.

His Aunt Eleanor refused to accept any visits from him, and he had no new leads to share with Sarah—meaning, unfortunately, no true reason to contact her. Instead of pursuing the mystery any further, he spent most of his time cooped up in his room at the bed and breakfast, avoiding the proprietor, Joshua, and keeping to himself.

Not so long ago, he'd been happy to lie low, read a book or two, find a show to binge on Netflix… but now he craved more.

Maybe he *should* get a dog. That is, if the inn would even allow pets. Or maybe it was time he put down actual roots. They didn't have to be here. He could go anywhere. He at least had enough money left to set up a home and find a new job to fill his days.

But how could he leave without knowing if Eleanor had told him the truth, if he really did have a whole side of the family he knew nothing about? Sure, a few extra cousins, aunts, and uncles wouldn't change much—but he'd be less lonely, or at least *less alone* in this world.

Then there was sweet, sweet Sarah Campbell.

As ridiculous as it seemed, he missed her.

But how could he miss someone he hardly knew? And why did it feel like he'd been missing her even before they met?

A sudden cry of pain drew Finch's attention away from his thoughts, followed by several sharp barks. He rushed out to the main living area where he found Joshua lying on the ground and wincing in pain.

"What happened?" Finch asked, offering the other man his hand.

Joshua attempted to pull himself up but drew back with a strangled look on his face. "Twinged my back. Am I really that old?"

His dog Charlie stood nearby, waiting to make sure his human would be all right. Finch didn't know dogs well enough to tell if he was happy to be of service to his human or worried about the fall. Maybe it was both.

"Don't look at me like that," Joshua scolded the dog. "This is your fault, you know."

"Mine?" Finch said, still trying to make sense of what had happened.

"No." Joshua's tried to sit up again and grunted. "Charlie's. We're supposed to go to Dr. Keller's today for his yearly shots, but Charlie knew exactly what I had planned and refused to come out from his hiding spot under the desk. Yeah, he hates the vet that much. So I tried to pick him up and carry him. He struggled, my back went, and now here I am, lying face up on the ground."

Finch had never heard Joshua say so much at one time, least of all to him. Poor guy, especially seeing as only Finch was around to offer any help. He'd long ago proven how useless he was when it came to emergencies, and the last thing he needed was for the innkeeper to die or become seriously injured on his watch.

Finch hesitated, trying to push his fears aside. "Are you okay? Do you need me to call someone?"

"Say that again." Joshua cupped a hand to his ear, reminding Finch that he was mostly deaf.

"Should I call someone for you?" Finch shouted.

"No, I'll be fine. Just give me a moment." He reached toward his dog who whined and laid down at his side. Joshua grasped Charlie's harness and rolled himself over onto his side, grunting in pain as he did.

Finch hovered nearby, not sure what his role in any of this should be.

Suddenly, Joshua laughed. "Oh, hey, will you look at that? There's my missing pen."

Finch followed the direction of Joshua's pointed finger and retrieved the missing writing instrument.

"Thanks," Joshua said and tucked it in his pocket. "That's my lucky charm. Went missing weeks ago and I'm afraid my luck went with it. Proves sometimes you just need a new perspective."

A new perspective. Yes! That's exactly what Finch needed. Besides, it made for the perfect excuse to see Sarah.

"Are you sure you're okay?" he asked Joshua one more time, eager to call Sarah and even more eager to see her again.

Joshua raised both arms and allowed Finch to pull him fully to his feet. "There. Good as new. Now, c'mon, you naughty dog."

Once Finch was sure the innkeeper wasn't going

to take another tumble, he pulled out his phone and texted Sarah: *We need a new perspective. Meet me at Cliff Walk in an hour.*

Chapter Ten

JUST AS SARAH had started to accept the fact that she might never see Finch Jameson again, a text message flashed across her phone. He'd invited her out to Cliff Walk, one of the most romantic destinations in all of Redwood Cove—and he'd also said something about needing a new perspective.

Could it be…? Had he decided to put Eleanor's mystery aside in favor of getting to know Sarah in a different way? Or was she reading too much into the situation?

Probably that. Because no matter how much Sarah swooned for Finch, he was still way out of her league—and any romantic entanglement was out of the question as far as her life plan was concerned.

But then why did her heart leap at the very sight of him? And why had she rushed to join him the moment he called for her?

Finch stood waiting at the trailhead with a pair of bottled waters and a placid expression. Lucky pranced merrily ahead, letting out a puppy whine before slathering Finch in kisses. His tail wagged so hard, it shook his entire body like a crazy balloon man flapping in the breeze outside a car dealership. Normally, he only greeted Sarah with such enthusiasm—and only when they'd actually been apart first.

"I missed you too, buddy." Finch laughed as he and Lucky continued to greet each other with such familiarity that it gave Sarah the spooks.

"Hi, Finch," she said shyly, hoping to high heavens that her cheeks weren't glowing red with embarrassment… or something worse.

He gave Lucky one last pat, then straightened to his full height, a good half foot taller than Sarah. "Thanks for coming."

"Yeah." If she wasn't blushing before, then she definitely was now that he'd turned the full wattage of his smile on her. "Umm, you mentioned a new perspective?"

"Yeah, sometimes I come up here to think, and since two heads are better than one…" He handed her a bottle of water as a pair of joggers breezed past—a man and a woman, a couple from the looks of it. Would she and Finch be like them one day? Meeting after work for a quick burst of exercise, then heading home to tuck in together for the night? The idea excited her more than she cared to admit.

"Sounds like a plan." She snapped Lucky's leash to his collar. Although he was normally perfect off leash, the Cliff Walk sometimes attracted bikers and Lucky just couldn't resist giving chase to the zippy two-wheel vehicles.

They walked side by side down the path which started out wide, but Sarah knew it would soon narrow, pushing them closer together. They'd only been apart for a matter of days, but already all the confidence she had built up while in his presence had been totally depleted. It was almost like meeting him again for the first time.

"I'll never get sick of the ocean," Sarah murmured as they broke through the brush to a clear view of the open water gleaming far below. Her tongue felt like a dry sponge, making it difficult to push the words out.

"Aren't you from close by?" he asked as his hand accidentally brushed against hers.

Sarah gently moved her hand away. As much as she loved the feeling of his skin on hers, it turned her brain to mush. And whether they were here to talk about the mystery or to talk about themselves, she needed all her wits about her tonight.

"I grew up in Ohio," she explained once she could function again. "No ocean there."

"What brought you here?" Another brush of skin. This time it didn't feel like an accident.

"Just… *life*." She didn't talk about her grandmother with anyone. Even though her parents never blamed her for what had happened on her watch, she felt their judgment, their sadness, with each visit —which is why they'd grown increasingly rare over the years.

"Fair enough. Well, as you probably already know, my family has been in California for generations, and I guess it never occurred to me to leave even when I had no family left to stay for."

Lucky stopped walking and grew very still. His ears perks up and he started to shake and whine softly. A moment later, he let out a loud bark and began to pull and strain against his leash.

Sarah followed the direction of her dog's gaze,

and sure enough… "Whales," she told Finch, pointing out to sea.

Finch took a step forward, so close she could feel the energy pulsing from his skin. For a moment, she was tempted to reach out and touch him. She rarely made physical contact with people who weren't her patients, weren't dying.

"Where?" he asked, squinting into the sun.

"Just wait. They'll breech again." She smiled, feeling in control again. The whales were a sign. They just had to be.

With another burst of water, a sleek pod of black and white bodies broke the surface.

"See?" Sarah said reverently. "Orcas. They're pretty much here year-round, you know."

Finch bumped his shoulder into hers playfully. "I thought *I* was supposed to be the local expert."

She shrugged and giggled despite herself. "Apparently not."

They stood side by side and watched the orcas until they had swum out of sight. Finch even snapped a few pictures, both of the whales and of Lucky's response to them.

"That was…" he said, turning to her.

"Magical," someone said from behind them both. Apparently a group of other hikers had gathered around to watch, even though Sarah had felt as if she and Finch were the only two people in the entire world.

"I thought I recognized one of my pups," Lucky's breeder, Carol Graves, said, marching up to them and extending her hand toward Finch. Lucky's parents, Rita and Sunny, walked obediently at her side despite the fact that she only held the leash joining them by her pinky finger.

"I'm Finch," Sarah's companion offered with a smile.

"Hi, Finch. I'm Carol. And who might this stranger be?" She turned toward Sarah with an exaggerated pout.

Oh, right. She'd deleted her Reel Life account. It had only been four or five days, but of course Carol had noticed.

She felt her cheeks grow hot, the majesty of the moment now lost entirely. "Sorry, I'll call you later tonight. Okay?"

"Oh, I see." Carol's voice took on a syrupy tone and she actually had the audacity to wink at Sarah. "I'm interrupting… something."

"No," Sarah insisted too quickly, drawing skeptical looks from both Finch and Carol. "It's not like that. We're just working together."

Carol continued to give Sarah a series of bemused looks. "Working? For the Rest Home all the way out here?"

"Something like that," she whispered, hoping that either Carol would leave or that she herself would die before the embarrassment could get any worse.

"Hey, Carol," Finch shot in, just as it seemed Carol was finally going to be on her way. "Since you're here, we may as well ask... Do you know anything about Bayside General Hospital?"

"Bayside General? *Hmm*." Carol shifted her weight to the side and brought a hand to her chin as she thought. "I went there years ago with a broken leg, but I tend to stay away if I can."

"Because you don't like hospitals?" Finch provided, his eyes widening as he waited for whatever potential clue Carol was about to reveal.

"Well, not much. I mean, who does? But that one in particular..." Her voice dropped several notches, taking on an eerie tone Sarah had never heard from her before. "Let's just say I know the scandal was before my time, but renaming the place isn't enough to make me forget what happened there."

Finch and Sarah exchanged quick glances. "What happened there?" they asked in unison.

Carol laughed. "Actually, it's been so long I can't remember exactly what it was, just that it was really bad."

Sarah felt the thrill of the mystery rising in her once again. "Do you remember what the hospital used to be called before?"

"Yeah, give me a second here." Carol motioned for both of her dogs to sit, then reached for her phone as if she could simply ask Siri for the answer. "It was one of those really generic names like Mercy or St. Something," she continued before her entire face lit up with triumph. "Oh, St. Mary's. That was it! I liked that it was named for a woman. Lot of good that did it."

"Yes, *yes*! Thank you so much for your help," Finch said, saddling Carol with an impromptu hug.

Now the old breeder was blushing. *Ha!* "Not sure what exactly I did to help, but glad you seem so happy. I'll let you two get back to it. Oh, and Sarah?" she added the last bit while adjusting her shirt and fluffing her hair.

"Yeah?" Sarah braced herself for whatever ribbing Carol had planned for her next. What she didn't expect was the warm hug and soft words that followed.

"We miss you on the Reel Life group chat. Come back soon."

AS SOON AS Carol left them in the clearing, Finch grabbed his phone and typed "St. Mary's of San Francisco" into the search engine. A flurry of results popped up featuring headlines that included scandal, shock, and murder. Finch scrolled down a ways, then clicked on one that linked to some kind of local history website.

"What is it?" Sarah asked, drawing closer, Lucky's leash wrapped tightly around her fist.

Finch suppressed a shudder and read aloud:

"To this day, the St. Mary's Murder remains one of the most infamous, but least talked about, cold cases in California history."

"Murder?" Sarah worried her lip, looking to Finch for more.

A shiver ran through him as he continued to skim the article. "Here it is," he said, zooming in to make the text even larger.

"Although a young man of good health, Dr. Karda was found dead in the maternity ward at approximately 2:20 on the morning of December 14, 1955. The autopsy would later reveal he ingested a large quantity of..."

He stumbled over the unfamiliar drug names, then looked up at Sarah, his own shock reflecting back at him in her eyes.

"He was poisoned. But why?" She tucked into his side as they both stared down at the phone in disbelief.

Why had he insisted on pursuing this, and why had Eleanor knowingly sent them toward such a gruesome case? Would they face dangerous repercussions if they dug too deep? If anything happened to Sarah, he would never forgive his aunt… or himself.

Finch continued through the article quickly, unsure of how much more he could handle just now. "It says here that Dr. Karda was widely known as Dr. Death. His infant mortality rate was more than three times the average of others in the hospital. People started to suspect…"

"That he was killing newborns?" Sara's voice caught in her throat, and he wondered if she might start to cry. If he might also shed some tears. "That's awful."

"I don't think it was on purpose." Finch stuffed his phone back into his pocket, unable to look at it any longer. "Either he was really bad at his job or really un—"

"Lucky," they said together.

The Golden Retriever barked happily at the mention of his name and tried to tug them back down the trail.

"Or," Sarah said after a thoughtful pause, not taking Lucky's bait. "Something else was going on."

"Like what?" he asked, unable to make any sense of this new information within the context of the larger mystery. Maybe when the shock wore off, the pieces would rearrange themselves into a clearer picture…

Sarah shook her head, letting Lucky's leash go slack. "I don't know, but I have a feeling we both know someone who does."

"Eleanor." He pictured the hostile old woman who had turned his life upside down, but he'd also introduced her to Sarah… "She's been refusing my visits."

"Well, lucky for you, you have a friend who can get you in anyway." Sarah grabbed his hand and turned them back toward the start of the trail. Even though she immediately let go, he felt her lingering grip as the ocean wind continued to breeze past. She was softening to him again. He felt it as sure as the sky was blue.

"Friends?" he teased, loving the taste of the word on his tongue. "Not just partners in crime?"

She shrugged, already losing some of her newly gained bravado. "That okay with you?"

Finch thought about this. He wanted to be so much more than friends with this girl, but he also didn't want to push her faster than she could handle. He grabbed her hand again and squeezed it in his own. "For now," he told her, making sure she caught his signature smile before looking away.

NIGHT HAD ALREADY BEGUN to set in by the time they traced their way back down the trail and drove over to the Redwood Cove Rest Home. Sarah needed to use her employee key card to get them through the front doors.

"Are you sure she'll be happy to see us?" Finch asked as he followed her down the hall. This was only the second time he'd set foot in the facility. It felt strange that so much had happened since his last visit.

Sarah made a noise that was halfway between a chuckle and a sigh. "Actually I'm pretty sure she won't be, but maybe we can catch her off her guard. Maybe she'll actually tell us something worth knowing this time." She rapped on the patient's door before sending Lucky in ahead of them.

"To soften her up a bit," she whispered to Finch by way of explanation.

"I know you're out there, and I don't want to see either of you," Eleanor called from within the dark room.

Finch flicked the heavy switch on the wall, bringing in a sudden burst of fluorescent light.

Eleanor groaned. "Can't I sleep without being

harassed?"

Finch plopped himself onto the end of her bed, unwilling to be ignored. "You told us to find the truth, set things straight, and so here we are."

"So you found your true family?" She refused to look at him, settling instead for keeping her eyes firmly shut as they spoke.

"Not yet, "Finch admitted. "But we know about the murder."

"Know what exactly?"

"Umm, that it happened."

"And under suspicious circumstances," Sarah added quietly, still standing in the doorframe and watching the scene unfold from a distance.

Eleanor laughed bitterly, then broke apart in a coughing fit. "I'm surprised it took you this long to find that little tidbit that was splashed all over the news. Even with grossly lacking research skills as you seem to have, you should have been able to find that on day one. At least tell me you found the killer."

"What? *No.* That's why we came to see you." The old woman's laughter set him on edge. Finch had already been mocked more than his fair share by the media, and he refused to let Eleanor add to it. He'd come here to help *her*, for crying out loud!

"If I wanted to spoon-feed you every last detail, I would've done that to begin with. Now go away and leave me alone." She flicked her wrist nimbly, shooing him away as if he were a naughty animal and not a human being.

"*No*," Finch answered, refusing to budge from his spot on the bed. "You're not some queen who can hand off orders from on high. It's clear you have the answers we need, so just spit them out already."

Sarah sucked in a deep breath.

Lucky sat and waited.

Finch held his ground.

At last, Eleanor groaned and strained to sit up in her bed.

And for one blissful moment he thought she might actually cave…

But in the next moment she was pressing the call button and bringing the night shift nurse scuffling into the room.

"Is everything okay here, Ms. Barton?" the nurse asked with a worried glance toward Sarah and Finch.

"No, it's not," Finch answered hotly. "And at this rate I doubt it ever will be."

Chapter Eleven

SARAH ARRIVED at work the next day with a small gift for Eleanor. Because the old woman enjoyed Lucky's company far more than any human's, Sarah had selected a cute plush Golden Retriever to give her as something of a peace offering. She hoped Eleanor would see the kindness of this gesture and not be irritated that stuffed animals were generally meant for children.

After all, everyone could use more softness in their life, especially someone with as many hard edges as Eleanor Barton.

"Good morning!" she sang brightly as she rounded the corner to Eleanor's room.

The nearby orderly regarded her with a sorrowful expression, not returning the greeting.

Never mind. Sarah had a good feeling about today. Each day was a new beginning, a new chance to get things right. And today she would try speaking with Eleanor with respect and kindness—and *without* Finch. Surely the old woman would open up then.

She took a deep breath before bounding into Eleanor's room. "Hell... *oh!*"

Fear and confusion gripped her heart. The room lay completely bare. The bed had been stripped and Eleanor herself was nowhere to be seen. In Sarah's line of work, that could only mean one thing...

Tears stung at the corners of her eyes as the realization struck her. *No.*

After placing the stuffed toy on Eleanor's empty bed, Sarah rooted in her pocket for a tissue with which to dry her eyes. Had Finch's and her prying been the final straw? They should have left her alone like she asked. They shouldn't have...

A small, cold hand fell on Sarah's shoulder from behind. *Mrs. Cheung. The facility director.*

"Is she...?" Sarah turned toward the dark-haired woman who commanded great authority despite her diminutive size.

Mrs. Cheung shook her head subtly and moved her hand to Sarah's elbow. "Come with me."

"I can't believe this," Sarah said as they walked together down the long hall. "I was just with her yesterday, and now? I had no idea she was so close to the end. She seemed so… *feisty*."

"Have a seat, Sarah," the director said once they'd reached her office.

Sarah settled herself into the upholstered visitor's chair and crossed her legs at the ankles. The office was at least five degrees warmer than the rest of the facility, giving it a slightly suffocating air. Rarely were staff called into the office. Mostly this space was used to meet with prospective residents and their families. In fact, the last time Sarah had been here was when Mrs. Cheung had offered her a raise to her yearly salary.

Could that be the case today?

Her eyes drifted to the framed family pictures that lined Mrs. Cheung's desk. A cheerful daisy toy danced in the sunlight filtering through the large windows behind them.

Mrs. Cheung folded her hands in front of her before speaking. "Sarah, you've done good work for us, and I've enjoyed having you here. Unfortunately, there's no easy way to say this, but… we've received a pretty serious complaint and have to put you on suspension during the investigation."

Whatever Sarah had expected to hear, it certainly wasn't this. A complaint? And suspension? *How? Who?*

Mrs. Cheung pushed a paper across her desk and into Sarah's shaking grip. "Here's a formal writeup of the complaint. I'm sure you understand our hands are tied here."

Sarah glanced down at the document, still reeling with shock. Two words jumped off the page and slapped her right in the face: *Eleanor Barton.*

She continued reading quickly, her lips moving along with the words she couldn't believe had landed her in front of her. "She's accusing me of elder abuse?" she asked in a cracking voice.

Mrs. Cheung cleared her throat. "*Accusing* is a strong word, but yes. She gave her statement earlier this morning and asked to be moved to Gold Coast General for her safety."

"I just... I can't believe this," Sarah cried. She wanted to shout at the injustice, but all her energy was still going toward trying to understand how this could have happened, why Eleanor would beg for her help and then try to ruin her life like this.

"I was surprised, too," the director admitted. "But the protocol is very clear when it comes to allegations of abuse. We'll need your ID card for now. When our investigation is complete, you can come back to work, provided…"

"Yeah, I get it." Sarah unclipped her badge and flung it across the desk.

"It's not personal," Mrs. Cheung murmured. "It's just the way we have to do things."

Sarah nodded, her tears flowing freely now. How could she ever expect to come out on top if she insisted on following the rules while others bent them freely? And how could she help Eleanor Barton if the old woman insisted on making an enemy of her?

With nothing left to say, she shuffled out of the office and into the bright sunshine outside. Just moments before, the sunny day had lifted her spirits. She felt as if she were on a collision course with the giant ball of fire. How long would it be now before the rest of her world came crashing down around her?

FINCH AWOKE EARLY the next morning. He'd spent much of the night tossing and turning with rage and still felt angry upon waking. Just who did Eleanor think she was to push this mystery off on

him? If it was so important to her, then why
wouldn't she help? And if it wasn't important, why
get him and Sarah involved in the first place?

The more he thought about it, the less sense
it made.

Part of him wanted to scrap the whole thing
and get on with his life, but the larger part understood there wasn't much of a life to get back to.

So he grabbed a quick shower and shave and
headed to the local police department on the off-
chance they might be more free with their records
than the hospital had been. He even swung by
Sweets and Treats to grab some of Grace's famous
giant donuts to offer up as a friendly bribe.

On the way, a bright red sign caught his eye.
FOR SALE. He stopped to study the empty store-
front where a pair of mannequins stood abandoned
in the window. Had this once been a dress shop?

He hadn't noticed the vacant building before,
and he wasn't entirely sure why he'd noticed it now.
For a moment, he let himself fantasize about
opening up a photography studio where he could
take pictures of people's babies, pets, and gradu-
ating seniors. It would be nice to have a purpose
again, something to look forward to each day. And
this would be the perfect spot for it.

Maybe when the Eleanor thing was resolved he'd come back and put in an offer. He smiled to himself. This was the first time in a long while he'd put thought into the future. Perhaps it could still be bright after all.

Finch forced himself to keep moving. If it were meant to be, the lease opportunity would be here later when he was ready for it. For now, he had other, more annoying things to take care of.

Thankfully, the officers at the Redwood Cove first precinct were quite happy to see him when he strode in with two jumbo donuts and a tray of fresh coffees.

"Thank God for stereotypes," a detective with salt and pepper hair and a handlebar mustache smacked between bites. "Otherwise no one would ever think to bring us treats like this!"

Finch gravitated toward the plump and jolly officer who was not too unlike how he might have pictured Santa Claus as a slightly younger man.

"I'm investigating a cold case," he said, cutting to the chase. "Was wondering if you might be able to help fill in some of the details."

"Ahh, so you're a P.I." The officer shoved another bite of donut into his mouth with glee.

Finch shrugged. "Something like that."

"What case you looking into?" He seemed nice enough, but not very interested. Finch needed to find a way to get him hooked, if there was to be any chance of finding help with the PD.

He tried to sound casual, knowing that if he spoke with too much enthusiasm he'd come across as some crazed hobbiest. "Well, it happened a long time ago, but I have reason to think my family might have been involved."

The officer leaned back in his chair and put both arms behind his head, settling in for the long haul. "Oh, this is going to be good," he said with renewed interest in Finch's plight.

"Have you heard of the St. Mary's Murder? It happened in the 50's."

The detective stretched his legs and laughed. "Yeah, of course. Everyone's heard of that one. It's actually one of the cases they train the new kids on these days."

Jack smiled. He knew his grin had a placating effect on women but wasn't sure how far it would get him with this manly officer. Still, anything that could help was worth a try. "Is there anything you can tell me that might help me solve it?" he asked.

The policeman laughed and, despite appearances, it sounded nothing like Santa Claus's merry trill. "You think you can solve a case more than sixty years old when dozens and dozens of professionals haven't learned a thing about it in all that time? Thanks for the laugh and the donuts. I needed both this morning."

Finch crossed his arms and stared the other man down. So his attempts at kindness had failed. Regardless, he would not be mocked. "I'm glad you think it's so funny, but seeing as you've all failed to finish the job, someone has to do it."

"Oh ho ho!"

Finch didn't care for this cruel, uniformed version of Santa at all.

"Think you know better than us, do you?" He reached into his desk drawer, still laughing feverishly. After scribbling a website down on a piece of spiral notebook paper, he tore the page off and handed it to Finch.

When Finch tried to take it, the officer ripped it away again. "Not so fast."

Finch rolled his eyes. He refused to let this man's ribbing get to him, but still, he needed whatever information was on that paper.

"If you actually do somehow manage to solve this thing, *I* get the credit. Got it? Okay, here's my card." He waited for Finch to accept the business card before finally offering over the paper.

"Seriously, good luck to you," the officer, whose name appeared to be Carerra, called after him before erupting in laughter once more.

Good grief.

Finch hurried out of the station, already subjected to enough humiliation for the day. When he finally glanced down at the paper, he saw that the web address belonged to the exact same cold case site he'd already found via yesterday's Google search.

So much for calling in the pros…

Chapter Twelve

AT A LOSS, Sarah wandered around town after being dismissed from work. She tried calling Finch, but it went straight to voicemail. Unfortunately, she didn't have anyone else to call or anywhere else to go…

How pathetic.

"What are we going to do now, Lucky?" she asked her faithful companion, but the dog didn't have any more answers than she did.

Why did it suddenly feel as if everything in her life had been taken away? Perhaps it was because Eleanor's accusation stung her in the most sensitive area of her heart.

Her grandmother.

Sarah's negligence.

A death that needn't have happened.

And now the same thing was happening again.

Why had she ever thought she could repent for what she'd done so many years ago? How could she possibly expect to alleviate a conscience that had long been buried beneath an overwhelming mass of guilt? She couldn't even begrudge Eleanor her lies. Sarah had pushed too hard for information— she'd let Finch push too hard.

Now they'd never have answers, and Sarah's work reputation would forever be tainted. Would the other staff and patients assume Eleanor's claims her true? Would they treat Sarah differently from now on?

Everything about this situation hurt. Sarah's job was all she had besides Lucky, and…

Her phone jangled with an incoming call. *Finch.*

His words tumbled out quickly, brightly. He still didn't know. "Sorry I missed your text. I was at the police station, trying to—"

Sarah cut him off with a racking sob. She just couldn't keep it in anymore.

Finch's voice immediately turned tender. "Whoa, hey. What's wrong?"

"I..." How could she possibly explain what happened? Finch would feel guilty, no doubt, and that was the last thing she wanted.

"Did something happen at work?" he prompted, his voice still soft, concerned.

Sarah nodded even though she knew he couldn't see, then finally managed, "I got put on suspension."

"What? Why? Wait..." Now the words weren't soft. They'd become sharp with vitriol. "This was Eleanor, wasn't it?"

Sarah nodded again. "Yes, and I don't know why. I thought..." The tears fell faster.

Finch's voice sounded a million miles away, and she wished more than anything that he was right here with her now. "I am so sorry. I'm going to take care of this, but first, I want to take care of you. Where are you?"

"Downtown by the bakery." Sarah sniffed. Finch couldn't fix this, but he could at least help her feel better. Hopefully.

"I'm not too far from there. I'm coming to get you. Is Lucky with you, too?"

"He's always with me," she replied matter-of-factly.

"Right, of course. See you in five." He hung up before Sarah could say goodbye.

And not even three minutes later, Finch's understated sedan appeared at the curb. "Hop in," he said, rolling down the window and waiting for her and Lucky to join him inside.

"Thanks for coming to get me," she whispered, her voice husky from all the tears she'd already shed that day. "I still can't believe your aunt would—"

"Nope," Finch cut her off. "We aren't going to talk about her."

Sarah moaned. Without the option to talk about his aunt, the two of them had nothing in common. She needed this in order to keep Finch close without allowing him to get too close. "But the mystery…"

"We aren't going to talk about that, either." He shook his head and placed a chastising finger to his lips.

"Then?"

"We both need a break. Don't you think?"

"What do you mean? Are you taking me home? My car is at—"

"Nope. We need to do something fun just for us. No murder mysteries, no bitter old ladies, just us.

And Lucky," he added, reaching back to pat the Golden Retriever on his head.

Sarah settled back in her seat and let out a shaky breath. "That sounds nice," she admitted.

"Good. Because I like you, Sarah Campbell, and I want you to feel better." That was the first time either of them had admitted their feelings to the other, and with it, something shifted in Sarah's heart. It had been a long time since she'd been in mutual like with a boy—let alone a man—and she didn't have the slightest idea how to respond.

"You like me?" she asked, her voice heavy beneath the weight of these three tiny, yet mighty, words.

"Very much." And then he flashed one of his award-winning smiles her way, giving her not just butterflies but an entire sky full of winged creatures in her belly.

She gulped. "Do you mean...?"

"*I mean* you're an amazing woman and you don't deserve to feel this way. So, let's go have some fun and get you smiling again." His ocean eyes drew her in, made her never want to look away.

She didn't feel very amazing that day, but she felt miles better with Finch at her side. "Okay," she said. "Let's go have some fun."

This time, she didn't worry about what he might have planned, whether it jived well with her straight-laced lifestyle or whether it would get them in trouble. She simply let go and trusted him to deliver his promise of a day well spent.

A day together.

For better or worse.

FINCH AND SARAH waited rather impatiently in line for the Go Carts. The few times she tried to direct the conversation back to Eleanor and the mystery, he redirected her by asking pointed questions about Lucky. He was beginning to know more about the dog than the girl, which definitely wouldn't do.

"You ready to lose, Campbell?" Finch teased, ready for this day to at last be about the two of them and nothing else.

"What? You aren't going to let me win?" she shot back, nudging his foot with hers. Why did a kick from Sarah feel better than any caress from his previous girlfriends?

"Not on your life." He already felt as if he had won just by being in this wonderful woman's company, but he wasn't about to say something so overtly corny and put her off.

Just then, their turn came up, and the cart jockey motioned them toward a pair of waiting vehicles.

"You look cute in that helmet," Finch offered, after shoving his onto his head and lowering the visor.

"Funny, because you don't." She stuck out her tongue at him before pulling down her visor as well.

"Oh, it's on!"

All this flirting was driving Finch crazy in the best of ways. Why couldn't every day be like this?

One of the nearby employees held onto Lucky's harness at the outside of the track. The dog barked when Finch glanced his way.

"Ready?" The trackmaster asked, waiting for nods from both Sarah and Finch.

And when he got them, he shouted, "Go!"

Finch pressed down hard on his gas pedal, jolting the little car to life. It had been years since he last drove one of these small, zippy vehicles, but he still had no trouble navigating the twists and turns in the track.

As he finished his first lap, he searched around for Sarah—and found she'd collided head-on with one of the barriers. Finch laughed and waved as he passed.

"I'll get you next time!" she shouted, shaking her fist like some kind of old-timey cartoon character.

By the time Finch lapped the track again, Sarah's cart had been restored and she was quickly gaining speed. "That's more like it," he called. "You're finally going to give me some competition here!"

Sarah kept both hands on the wheel, predictably, safely, at ten and two. "Don't talk to me while I'm driving!" she shouted, pulling slightly ahead of him.

Finch laughed so hard, he lost focus and—*crash!* He ended up bouncing off the barrier wall himself.

"Did you have fun?" he asked her once they were both back on their feet. The ground still felt as if it were buzzing beneath him and he had to hold onto a handrail to steady himself as he pulled himself away from the track.

"I had fun watching you crash," she answered with a laugh and a playful jab.

"Yeah, yeah, laugh it up while you have the chance. I bet you won't be laughing when we hit the zip line."

Sarah blanched. "The zip line? Um, no thanks."

He grabbed her hand, and she reluctantly walked with him toward the next attraction. "Nope, you're not getting it out of it. Nobody comes to the adventure center without making the leap."

"Yes, *me*. I do."

"Two please," he told the man at the booth, handing him his card.

She crossed her arms over her chest, refusing to look at him. "No, Finch. I don't want to."

"But that's why you have to."

She risked a quick glance his way. "How do I know it's safe?" Her eyes were wide with fear, and he wanted so badly to take her in his arms and tell her it would be all right.

Instead, he had to settle for words. "I promise you it's safe. Look, I'll even go first," he said as the worker handed him a pair of harnesses. "Now, do you need me to help you get strapped in?"

"I guess." She let out a deep breath and stood rooted to the spot as Finch and the worker secured her in the safety harness.

Sarah said nothing more as they climbed to the top of the platform. Once they were up high with the wind whipping her hair against her neck, she asked, "Remind me why I'm doing this again?"

"Because sometimes in life you just have to take the leap."

Sarah laughed nervously. "That is so cliché. Just take the leap? Really, Finch?" She laughed harder, stumbled a bit to the side, then sobered up quickly as she grappled for the handrail at the edge of the platform.

"Okay, how about this," he said as the worker used a pair of strong carabineers to hook him to the line. "You're doing this because sometimes you just have to stop being afraid and go for it. Because sometimes you have to break the rules, defy gravity, in order to live a little. Now are you ready?"

Her knuckles had begun to turn white where she clutched to the guardrail. "I don't think I'll ever be ready…"

"Then that definitely means you should do it. Look, there are only two ways down. I know which way I'm taking." And with that, he jumped off the platform, letting the line carry him toward the mountains in the distance. There was the brief moment of thrill where he couldn't tell if the harness was attached, then the split-second of falling before the line caught him and sent him sliding down the cable like a diving falcon.

At the bottom, he caught himself running and unhooked the line as fast as he could, waiting to see if Sarah would be brave enough to follow. He'd almost given up on her when at last a shrill scream broke through the air and Sarah's emerging form quickly followed.

She half-screamed, half-laughed the entire way down as she flew through the clouds, his own personal angel. She missed catching her foothold at the bottom, but Finch was quick to reach out and steady her descent, running backward with her in his arms until they both stopped.

Sarah fit in his arms as if she'd always belonged there. He unhooked her helmet and let it drop to the ground, reaching to brush her hair from her face. She pressed her cheek into his hand and closed her eyes. Both of their hearts beat wildly.

Her lips parted as she waited.

The perfect moment had arrived, but was it really perfect? Sarah had been put on suspension from her work that day—and it was because of his deranged aunt. Would their first kiss be forever tainted if he were to take it now?

And why was he putting so much pressure on them? On himself?

He swallowed hard, praying he'd made the right choice as he set Sarah firmly back on the ground.

"There," he said with a disappointed smile. "Told you you'd like it. But next time you've gotta land on your own two feet instead of mine."

Chapter Thirteen

SARAH'S HEART SKIPPED A BEAT—AND not in the good kind of fairytale way, but more like a train sliding off the tracks and bursting into flames as it hurtled toward a bottomless sea.

Yup, that was exactly how she felt right about then. Her heart hammering an unsteady beat, her mind reeling, her world spinning off its axis...

Why didn't Finch kiss me?

The moment was perfect, both physically and metaphorically. He'd literally caught her when she'd fallen. Their faces were so close she'd been able to taste his salty skin with each bated breath.

But then he set her down and moved away so fast Sarah had to question what she'd eaten that day and whether any of it might still be lingering on her breath or in her teeth.

Mortified didn't even begin to cover it, especially since Finch seemed unaware of the disappointment that now stung every nerve ending in her body.

"Want to go again?" he asked after shoving both hands deep into his pockets and taking a step to the side.

Sarah shook her head, worried that if she tried to speak she might yell or cry or both. For just the briefest of periods she'd bought into his act, into the pretty picture he painted of putting fears aside and living in the moment.

What a crock.

At the end of the day, Finch would always be a businessman. He knew how to say what others wanted to hear whether or not he meant the words. Was he being honest when he told Sarah he liked her? When he flirted with her at the Go Carts? Or was he just trying to distract her from the whole mess with Eleanor?

And if he *did* want to distract her, then *why?* Were he and Eleanor in on some big joke together? Was there even a mystery, or did they both find enjoyment in messing with her brain and her heart?

Too many questions, and each of them hurt to ask—never mind the answers.

"Let's go grab some lunch," Finch said, reaching a hand toward her.

But she refused to take it. Instead, she forced a smile and followed a step behind as he led her over to the small outdoor eatery within the adventure center complex. She needed to figure out a way out of there before she could embarrass herself any further or let Finch cut her any deeper.

"Do you like fish tacos?" he asked, fiddling with his wallet as he studied the menu board.

"I guess." She pulled out her phone and pretended to check email. It would have been nice to mindlessly scroll through her Reel Life feed to help distract her thoughts, but no… she'd deleted it… and for him.

Finch finished ordering their food and sat down next to her on the picnic table bench.

When she looked up from her phone, she found him staring at her, his brows furrowed in confusion. *What's there to be confused about? You led me on. Or maybe I led myself on.*

He pushed the tray toward her and attempted a smile. "Is everything okay?"

She shrugged, hating herself for acting like a

pouty teenager but unable to form coherent, level-headed sentences until she sorted through her feelings.

"Is it about my aunt? The suspension?" he asked in a way that seemed to suggest he knew it wasn't—but perhaps hoped it was.

Sarah was let off the hook from answering his questions when Finch's phone trilled in his pocket. He slapped his hands against each other to brush off any stray crumbs, then pulled the device from his pocket.

"I don't recognize the number," he told her before clicking over to answer the call. "Hello?" His eyes widened as he listened, then he held his hand over the speaker and whispered, "Well, speak of the devil."

Sarah could only hear muffled whispered on the other end of the conversation. As Finch attempted to rush through his call, Sarah fiddled with her own phone, trying to think up an excuse that would get her out of there.

Finch nodded and rolled his eyes as the other speaker dominated the conversation. "Yes... Yes... Okay... Today?... Is it really that urgent?... Uh-huh... Yeah... Yes, I get it... Bye."

"Everything okay?" she asked once he'd hung up.

He frowned. "No, it's Eleanor. She needs me at the hospital for some reason…" He paused to let out an exhausted, dramatic sigh. "But I'm not going," he assured her, not knowing that she desperately wanted him to go—or at least to leave her.

Sarah immediately latched onto this. "Finch, you have to go. She needs you."

"How could you be so kind to her when she's only made trouble for you?"

Because I'm a catch, whether or not you realize it. Sarah shocked herself with this realization. She'd never thought of herself as worthy before. So why now?

She shrugged. Finch could think whatever he wanted about her. She just needed him gone. "It's just, she doesn't have anyone else," she explained. "And… And I got a text from work, asking me to come in, so—yeah."

"Okay, I mean, if you're sure. We can head over there after lunch."

"It sounded really urgent, and I'm not all that hungry. Why don't we go now?" Sarah stood before Finch had a chance to weigh in, and by the time he'd taken their trays to the waiting trash cans, she'd already made it halfway back to the parking lot.

HE SHOULD HAVE KISSED HER. Sarah's reaction made that much obvious.

Why did he have to go and try to be a gentleman? How had he managed to overread the situation and *still* reach the wrong conclusion?

The worst part was seeing how Sarah couldn't get away from him fast enough. He wanted to explain—or to grab her and kiss her right then—but he just couldn't do that. He needed to fix what had broken between the two of them before he could even dream of taking such a big leap forward in their relationship.

And then the hospital had called, practically pleading with him to visit his aunt.

Oh, he had hated her in that moment.

In fact, he hated her in most moments. *Oh, the joy of having a family!*

Sarah so quickly latched onto that escape hatch that he had little choice than to comply with the old bat's wishes. He knew she hadn't actually received a text calling her into work, but pointing that out would only mortify them both.

So he watched sadly as Sarah bounded out of his car with Lucky at her heels, his tail swinging along with the beat of their steps. This was it—time for the visit no one wanted to happen. Whether or not Eleanor had requested him, he already knew she wouldn't be happy to see him. Nothing ever made that woman happy.

Gold Coast General Hospital appeared practically vacant when he arrived. Maybe nobody got sick or had accidents this time of year, or maybe they all went somewhere else. Had this place also had a scandal he knew nothing about?

Finch charged through the halls toward the room number the nurse had given him. Before he could reach Eleanor, though, a lanky young man intercepted him.

"Hi, Mr. Jameson. It is Mr. Jameson, right? I recognized you from… Yeah, so thank you for coming. We need you to sign some paperwork for your aunt, if you'll just come with me."

Finch followed the squeaky voiced intern—he had to be an intern, because he couldn't have possibly been older than twenty-five—over to a nearby standing station and listened as he flipped through various items in a hastily assembled file folder.

"So this is the advance directive," he explained, pointing to the place where Finch needed to sign below Eleanor's signature. "It means if she stops breathing we won't implement life-saving measures."

Finch dropped the pen in surprise. "Is that what she really wants?"

"She already signed," the young man pointed out.

Finch shook his head and signed where instructed—first the advance directive and then a myriad of other forms, all of which seemed far less momentous after that one.

"Okey dokey, that oughta do it!" the intern sang, clicking the pen closed. "I won't keep you any longer."

Finch thought about leaving from there, his commitment met, but the watchful eyes of the hospital staffer bore into his back, judging before there was even anything to judge. Rather than escaping as he'd hoped, he skulked into Eleanor's room.

He found his great aunt seated in the bed near the window, her hands folded neatly in her lap. A little plush Golden Retriever lounged comfortably at her side. The toy seemed far too sweet for her, and he wondered briefly where she'd gotten it or why she would have kept it.

He cleared his throat, lingering in the doorway in hopes of escaping her overwhelming and often hostile gravitational pull.

"What are you doing here?" she asked with a rasp.

"The hospital called me. Wanted me to sign some forms."

"And you did?" She looked tired—far more tired than before. Her smooth complexion was now marred by deep, dark circles around her eyes, and her hair hadn't been curled—possibly also not brushed.

Finch nodded and ventured a step deeper into the room. Maybe this weakened version of Eleanor would play nice. Maybe she finally realized she needed him, after all. Maybe...

"Good." Eleanor turned her head back toward the window, but he could tell her attention was still focused on him despite how she wanted things to appear. A moment later, she sighed and snapped back his way. "Well, what do you want?"

So much for his theory about having a kind

encounter that day. "You know what I want," he said, staring her down while she did the same to him.

His great aunt laughed bitterly. "Yes, you've become rather predictable."

"Maybe *I* have, but not *you*…" The rage came flooding back. If he wasn't careful, he might drown in it one day. It took everything he had to keep from yelling at the frail, old woman right there in the middle of the hospital. "Do you know you cost Sarah her job?"

She shrugged and examined her nails. Did she really believe her chipped manicure was more important than Sarah's livelihood? "It was a means to an end," she replied coldly.

If Eleanor was ice, then Finch was definitely fire. He knew which of those elements came out on top when the two were forced together. He just had to stay strong—keep demanding justice, answers, respect. "What? Listen to you! How could you say that? All she has ever done is help you."

His words did nothing to melt her icy exterior. Perhaps her heart had died prior to the rest of her body. "And now she's helping me now by staying away."

"You're messing with people's lives, and you don't even care," Finch spat.

"I care plenty," she insisted, but her words held little passion and likely no truth, either.

"Could have fooled me." Finch was done playing her game. He still didn't understand her end goals, but he no longer cared.

"Believe what you want for now." Eleanor settled into her bed, pulling her blanket up higher on her chest. "The truth will come out eventually."

"Will it? Because I'm done with you and your stupid mystery. The more any of us tries to help you, the more merciless you become. I'm ending it here." Enough with the cryptic hints and the words that said nothing, the heart that felt nothing. He was nobody's pawn, least of all Eleanor Barton's.

"No, you're not," she insisted without hesitation. Apparently she still thought of herself as a queen. This only angered Finch more.

He turned to leave and even made it the length of a few rooms, but then something ignited inside of him. He couldn't let her have the last word. Couldn't let her think any of this was okay.

"Go ahead and believe whatever you want," he said with a raised voice, charging back into the room. He needed her to understand that they were really, really through. "Here's what I believe: you're sending Sarah and I all across the coast in search of answers when you know good and well you're the one behind that murder. You probably even liked watching him die, but now you're dying, so you're looking for some kind of divine forgiveness. Guess what? No one will ever forgive you. Especially not me. You're going to die guilty and alone, and it's going to be all your fault."

His piece said, Finch walked away from the only family he had left.

He was definitely better off alone.

Chapter Fourteen

SARAH SPENT the next few days locked snugly inside her house. She couldn't risk leaving and running into someone from work—or worse yet, *Finch*.

Lucky tried to comfort her for the first couple of days, but his boredom soon outweighed his sympathy. She couldn't even bring herself to look her most loyal friend in the eyes because every time she did, he wiggled his doggie eyebrows and let out a low, soulful whine.

"I'm sorry, boy," she said, and she really did mean it. "But we have to stay here."

Lucky would groan and then go lie down in his oversized basket where he would watch Sarah intently from across the room.

Even my dog thinks I'm messing up my life!

Finch tried calling her more than once, but she didn't have anything to say to him. At least not yet. Maybe after she'd had more time to cool down, to think about what she really wanted, she'd come to a different conclusion. But for now, her days were better spent alone. *Plus Lucky.*

She'd just finished watching an episode of some new baking show on Netflix when her phone buzzed with an incoming call. *What does he want now?*

When she saw that the caller wasn't, in fact, Finch, she begrudgingly picked up. A part of her liked that he kept trying, though she hated to lead him on. What if this wasn't right for her? What if it would never be right?

"Hello?" she answered rather dispiritedly.

"What have you been up to, girly?" Carol Graves shouted into the phone. Sarah's favorite dog breeder was in a weird place—young enough to use the newest technology but also old enough to assume she needed to scream in order to be heard through the phone line.

"Learning how to bake cake pops and unicorn cakes," Sarah answered, rubbing her ears to stop the ringing.

"Oh, bring me some!" Carol shouted again.

Sarah just barely had time to save herself from the second onslaught by whipping the phone away from her ear. "I said I'm learning, not that I'm doing."

"Well, *someone's* smarmy today," Carol spat, and Sarah could practically feel the moisture hit her cheek. "Does this have anything to do with that handsome billionaire boyfriend I saw you with the other day?"

Maybe she shouldn't have picked up the phone after all. "One, he's not my boyfriend, and two, he's definitely not a billionaire," she explained, though her patience was seriously wearing thin.

Carol tutted at Sarah's denial, then finally brought her voice down to a normal speaking level. "You think I don't recognize the founder of my favorite social network?"

Sarah sighed but decided not to correct the other woman. Doing so would likely lead to a lengthy discussion about Finch, and that was the last topic Sarah felt like discussing these days. So much so that she volunteered another uncomfortable topic of discussion. "I got suspended from work."

"Yes, yes, I heard." Sympathy filled her voice,

though not surprise as Sarah had expected. "Such a shame."

"Wait… you heard?" She hugged a throw pillow to her chest, feeling the weight of everything crashing down on her all over again.

"Of course I did. From that handsome billionaire of yours, no less."

Ugh. Sarah pinched the bridge of her nose, but it was too late to fight off the tension headache that had begun to build beneath her brow.

"He's really worried about you, you know," Carol prodded softly.

"Yeah, okay." Sarah tossed the pillow back onto the couch and punched it with all her might. And like everything else in her life, she hardly made a dent.

Carol began to yell again. "I'm being truthful here! What did you do to that poor boy?"

"Me? To him? No, that's not how it went down." She pictured Finch as he held her in his arms after that terrifying leap from the zip line, the slow, tension-filled moment when they almost kissed, and then… him moving away, rejecting her in that moment. Perhaps for all moments.

"Then what did happen?"

"He…" Sarah stopped herself, realizing how

stupid the argument was. *He didn't kiss me when I wanted to.*

"That's what I thought," Carol said with a disappointed tut-tut.

Sarah just didn't have the strength to argue anymore. Instead, she decided to ask a question that had always plagued her about her breeder friend. "Carol?"

"Yes, dear?"

"How come you never got married?"

Carol let out a wistful sigh. One of her dogs barked in the distance, and Lucky tilted his head in response. "I've thought about that long and hard," Carol answered after a lengthy pause. "And I'm not entirely sure why. I guess it's because no one ever made me love and hate them at the same time."

"You think love is… hate?" This was certainly a new definition, but lately Sarah had been battling so many new feelings she couldn't decide whether or not she agreed with Carol's assessment.

"It has to be, at least in part," the other woman insisted. "Otherwise, how can you appreciate the good without the bad? How can you know your feelings are real if they're never challenged?"

She had a point here, and she'd also described how Sarah felt about Finch perfectly. Of course, none of this made her any less confused. None of it changed the fact that he'd had the opportunity to kiss her and hadn't. *Ugh.*

"Are you happy, Carol? Are you happy living all alone?"

"But I'm not alone. I have the dogs. And I have you and the others. You're my family."

A family through work. That would be nice if, one, Sarah hadn't been suspended from her job and, two, all of her patients didn't die within a matter of years after she met them.

"Now will you give that nice boy a call?" Carol asked, hope lighting in her voice.

"I'll think about it," Sarah answered before ending the call and looking back toward Lucky.

She motioned for him to join her at the couch. "Do you want to see Finch?" she asked the attentive canine.

Lucky barked, whined, wagged his tail, and spun in a circle, then grabbed his leash from the hook by the door and waited.

Well, at least his feelings were clear.

Now Sarah just had to figure out her own.

FINCH LISTENED to the phone ring on an endless loop. It didn't even go to voicemail this time, so he hung up and tried one more time. He'd called Sarah every day that week without any luck, but he just wasn't ready to give up on her yet. Oh, how he hoped he wasn't irritating her!

When she actually picked up after the second ring, he felt so shocked he nearly fumbled his phone. "You're alive!" he shouted breathlessly.

"Yeah, I'm alive... and bored."

Lucky barked in the background, apparently agreeing with his owner's statement.

"How can I help?" Finch asked. His cheeks hurt from smiling so hard.

"I've been thinking a lot about Eleanor's mystery, and I think I have an idea." Okay, so they wouldn't be addressing their almost kiss or the fact she'd been avoiding him for nearly an entire week. Still, he was too happy to care.

"I told her we were done helping," he confessed, thinking back to their confrontation in the hospital so many days ago.

Sarah sighed in frustration. "Maybe you are, but I'm not."

"But she was awful to you!" Finch's chest clenched. Now that he had Sarah back, he didn't want to waste any more time helping that ungrateful old woman. He only wanted Sarah.

Her voice became soft, almost like a whisper. "Yeah, but it's kind of all I have right now. And I just… I need something."

"Are they still investigating you at work?" Finch hated that she'd had to face this alone when he so desperately wanted to be there to help her through this. He'd once lost everything, too. There was life on the other side, and since meeting Sarah, there might also be happiness waiting, too.

"No, I got cleared, but I took some vacation time so I could think." How long had this been, and why had no one informed him? They'd lost so many days when they could have been together, learning about each other, figuring out where things might take them.

Oh, he was infatuated with this Sarah Campbell. The last time he'd devoted so much passion to any one thing, Reel Life had been born. What could come of him and Sarah? He didn't know yet, but he had a feeling it would be even better.

"What have you been thinking about?" he asked, wondering how soon he could get her to agree to come see him.

But she wanted to keep the topic focused on his

dearly not-departed great aunt, because she answered with "Well, Eleanor's mystery, for one."

"And?" *Please say something else. Please give this poor, lovesick man some hope.*

"One thing at a time." Fabric swished on the other end of the line, and he pictured her pacing around the living room he'd yet to see. He wondered if her style might be more fancy or minimalist. Probably a mix of both with antiques lovingly kept in a glass curio case. She, no doubt, had a story for each one. Would he one day get to hear those stories? Get to see that living room with his own eyes?

"Look, I'm going to solve this thing with or without you," Sarah continued. "But I would rather it be with you."

If that's what it took, then that's what Finch would do. "Fair enough," he said, hoping the extra time would help him cool off a little rather than further igniting his infatuation. The last thing he wanted to do was scare her off. He'd never cared this much about what anyone thought. The fact that he regarded Sarah so highly both delighted and terrified him in equal measure.

"So are you in?" Sarah asked, drawing his focus

back to their conversation about Eleanor, of all things.

"Yeah, I guess I am." One thing at a time—just like she'd said. This was clearly important to her, which suddenly made it important to him once more, too.

He could hear the smile in Sarah's words when she spoke again. "Good. So I've been thinking. The hospital isn't the only place that keeps records. We could try the police, too." Her pace quickened as they dove deeper into the topic. While Sarah had become Finch's passion, Eleanor had become hers.

Whatever it takes, he reminded himself.

"I already did," he confessed, remembering his odd run-in with Officer Carrera. "I was going to tell you, but then…"

"I get it. What about the newspapers? Did you try them?"

"Only what I've found on Google, and there's not a lot that goes that far back."

"I have an idea," she said, her voice hitching on that last word. "Meet me at the community college in half an hour?"

Yes, they could meet. And they would. It was exactly what he wanted but putting one thing at a time would be so much harder when they stood face-to-face. He had to know if she felt the same way he did, and so he tiptoed around the topic, hoping she'd be the one to rush at it full-on.

"Sarah, wait…" He chose each word carefully as he continued. "Shouldn't we talk about what happened with us first?"

"Something happened with us?" she asked, but he could see through right her. She knew, and she'd been thinking about it, too.

"You *know* what I mean. After the zip line, we—"

"Nope, let's just get to the college and see about accessing their archives."

"But I want you to know that—"

"One thing at a time, remember?"

Did that mean solving Eleanor's mystery would open up the possibility of a relationship between them at last? And what would happen if Eleanor died before they'd figured out any of her nagging secrets?

Now, more than ever, Finch felt the time ticking away.

He would not—could not—fail.

Chapter Fifteen

FOR THE FIRST time since meeting him, Sarah arrived at a rally point before Finch—a small feat for which she felt extremely grateful. It meant she had the chance to sort through some of her feelings before the two of them finally came face-to-face.

She'd thought long and hard about her talk with Carol, about when you knew the feelings really meant something. Not just about how they applied to Finch, but rather *everything* in life.

She cared about few things enough to form strong feelings in either direction. Everything in her life was simply okay.

None of it stood out.

None of it left a mark.

But with Finch, she felt like she might want something deeper, stronger, and that terrified her. Hopefully their time apart had put things into perspective for both of them. She wanted to give Finch another chance, but it would be too hard to sort through their feelings for each other while also trying to unravel Eleanor's mystery.

One thing at a time.

She took a seat on a mossy stone bench beneath the shade of a thick tree. The bench appeared as if it had been there for ages—almost as if it had become a part of the larger oak beside it—and she wondered if both of them pre-dated the college. What had this place been before? Was it better now, or did the modern new campus displace something beautiful?

How could you ever really know if change would be wonderful or tragic?

This line of thinking terrified Sarah.

Here she stood at the edge of one of life's giant cliffs. She could leap, possibly fly. Or she could delay, lose her footing, and fall.

Was standing still even an option? Could it ever be again?

Something had changed inside her, and she still didn't know what it might be. Whether it was safe, whether she was worthy to hope, to trust, to love…

Her phone pinged with a message from Finch: *Stuck in traffic. Be there in 5.*

She smiled to herself. So her perpetually punctual partner in crime wasn't infallible after all. Somehow that made her feel better, as if things had changed for him, too. Maybe those changes would help them fit together better… or maybe it would mean they'd have an easier time moving apart and getting on with their respective lives.

A fat squirrel ran down the tree and scampered up to Sarah, sitting only a few feet away as his little nose and whiskers twitched. These college campus squirrels were quite bold. She almost never saw the animals elsewhere. Few were brave enough to approach a dog…

Except Lucky wasn't there.

She'd been in such a hurry to get to the college and move forward with the mystery—and, okay, to see Finch again—that she hadn't remembered to bring him.

How was that possible? She brought him everywhere. Why was this outing any different?

"Hey there, stranger," Finch said, appearing suddenly and sinking beside her on the worn bench.

Sarah practically jumped out of her skin. "You scared me!"

"Sorry, I came up from behind. The front lot was full... Hey, where's Lucky?"

"At home. Not allowed in the college." For some reason, she didn't want him to know she'd been so excited to come here with them that she'd forgotten her constant companion and broken her own rule about them spending time together only when chaperoned by the dog.

"Ahh, bummer. Well, it sure is good to see you again." Finch placed his hand on the bench between them and edged his pinky toward hers, perhaps checking to see what level of contact between them was okay now. Sarah almost let him grab her hand, lace his fingers between his own.

One thing at a time!

She shot to her feet, anxiously tucking a strand of hair behind each ear. "Let's get going!" she said, hating the false cheeriness in her voice.

Just as she'd feared, seeing Finch again brought all the same feelings flooding back so fast it was impossible to dam them up. Too late. The damage was done.

She couldn't reverse time, but there was still so

much she had to figure out about herself before she could figure out where things stood with them.

Somehow solving Eleanor's mystery had become tantamount to resolving all the other lingering questions in her life—where Finch fit in. Whether they could possibly share a future.

Well, she could figure those answers out later.

"ARE we even going to be able to get in?" Finch asked as they walked uphill toward the campus library. The sun hung high in the sky, not a cloud to be seen. It was truly the perfect day, making him wish he could invite Sarah to run away with him to the beach.

Putting pressure on her, though, would only increase her skittishness with him. It seemed every single time the two of them got together, her heart had been reset and he needed to earn her trust all over again.

They needed to stop coming up with excuses, stop saying goodbye. And as much as he despised his great-aunt, he now wanted nothing more than to solve her mystery. Doing so was the only way he'd get even the whisper of a chance with the most perfect woman he'd ever met.

When they reached the library, Sarah strode in confidently without waiting for him to hold the door for her. *So much for chivalry.*

"See?" she said with a small smile of triumph. "Easy peasy."

He couldn't remember where they'd left the conversation and what she meant, but he liked that it had made her smile. "How are we going to access the archives?" he asked, glancing around the bustling space.

Sarah reached into her pocket and pulled out a worn plastic card. "I took a class here last year. Still have my student login."

"I thought you finished school back east," Finch asked, raising an eyebrow in her direction. There was still so much about this woman he didn't know —so much he longed to discover.

"I did, but this was just an enrichment class, something fun to do after hours."

"Really? What did you take?"

Sarah shrugged as if her answer didn't matter, as if she wasn't the most interesting person he'd ever met. "My patients talk about the wars a lot, so I wanted to know more. That's all."

"You really go the extra mile for all of them," Finch said, placing a cautious hand on her arm. "It's not just Eleanor."

Sarah shivered and wrapped her arms around herself, looking away as she spoke. "I like giving them a friend when they don't really have much of anyone left. It's about respect and human decency more than anything."

"Well, I think it's incredible."

"Uhh, thanks." She attempted a smile, but still looked so sad. Why couldn't she take his compliments?

"Anyway," Sarah continued, obviously eager to get back on task. "We should be able to access the local paper archives through the digitized collections. If not, we can ask to see the microfiche."

"Was it really just one class you took? You kind of seem like a pro here."

"Two or three in history. A couple more in other disciplines."

"What oth—?"

"Nope, we're not going to talk about me," she said, already walking away from him. "We're going to figure out what your aunt wants us to know. *To the computers!*"

Finch brought a hand to his mouth to cover his

laugh. Sarah was like a dog with a rope toy—irresistibly adorable and also crazy stubborn. He trailed after her toward the nearby bank of computers and pulled up a chair to watch over her shoulder as she deftly logged in and navigated the school intranet.

"Here it is," she announced proudly, hovering her cursor over something called *The Gold Coast Collection*. "This has most of the area newspapers up until like 2010 and back to 1800-something. We should be able to find something to help here."

Her hands lingered over the keyboard for a few moments before she turned toward him and asked, "What should I search first?"

"Try the *St. Mary's Murder*."

Sarah nodded. "Got it."

Finch smiled to himself as Sarah used each of her index fingers to type in the search terms. It seemed she had more in common with her elderly patients than even she realized.

"Oh my gosh, there are dozens!" Sarah cried as she scrolled down the page studying the array of headlines. She read the first couple, which largely rehashed what they already knew.

Finch had a hard time reading over her shoulder and longed to lean in closer, but he wanted Sarah to feel comfortable. He wanted her to be able to solve this mystery since it clearly meant so much to her... even beyond helping Eleanor. And far more than he could understand.

"Hey," he interrupted, "why don't you log me in over here so we can divide and conquer?"

"Ooh, good idea! You take this one and keep reading. I'll boot up the other and start reading the results from the bottom." She came alive again now that she had something to focus on other than Finch. He wished she would be like this always, but getting to know each other better had made her more uncomfortable around him, not less. He needed to find a way to fix that...

They worked beside each other for the next hour or so, occasionally sharing little tidbits with one another. Ultimately, they reached the end of the results without finding any smoking gun to help solve their mystery.

Sarah's face fell. "Maybe it really is hopeless."

"Don't say that. We're just getting started. Besides you're with a tech genius, remember?" He flashed one of his famous smiles her way. His mother had always said he could sell water to a fish with that smile, and it seemed to work now. Sarah softened right before his eyes.

"So now you're a genius, are you?" she asked playfully.

"Just when it comes to Google and stuff."

"But this isn't Google," she said with a laugh. "It's the *Gold Coast Collection.*"

"Yeah, yeah, but it works pretty much the same, right?" He typed in Eleanor's name demonstratively. "We just need to figure out the perfect search term, and—"

"Finch, look!" Sarah put both her hands on the back of his chair and leaned over his shoulder to get a closer look at the screen.

When he turned, he saw that his throwaway search had resulted in a single result titled *Letter to the Editor.* "Wasn't 'editor' one of the words on that nonsense jumbled list?" he asked, hardly able to believe their dumb luck.

Her eyes shone with anticipation. It was the happiest he had ever seen her... Well, other than right before their almost kiss at the zip line.

"Here," she said, unfolding the list after she removed it from her purse and pointing to the part that read:

1103563307924188,   *Editor,*
290257129312493942.

Dying of curiosity now that they finally had a lead, Finch clicked on the result and began reading:

Dear Editor:

I'd like to call out the utter lack of journalistic integrity in your article titled "Dr. Death's Murderer Still At Large 2 Years Later" that ran on February 29, 1957.

Sarah interrupted him by squeezing down on his shoulders before he could read any farther. "Finch!" she cried. "Look at the date!"

He re-read the last part. "February 29, 1957. Yeah, so?"

She sighed and pulled the paper from Eleanor out of her pocket again. "Look at this. *Really look at it,"* she said, thrusting it at him.

He read through the list slowly, carefully, and still at a loss.

She signed again and pointed to the word "editor" in the list, and then the string of numbers that came immediately after it. "See, it starts 29-02-57. That could mean the twenty-ninth of February 1957."

Sarah paused, apparently waiting for him to connect the dots. When he didn't, she rolled her eyes, let out a huff, and continued, "Which was the publication date of the article referenced in her letter to the editor. Don't you see? That can't be a coincidence!"

"Then what do the rest of the numbers mean. *12-93-12-49-39-42…*"

"I don't know. Keep reading," she urged him.

He nodded and read the rest of the letter aloud, wondering what else they were about to discover:

I had the honor of working with Dr. Karda for a time, and he was a good man who always did right by his patients. Continuing to call him Dr. Death even after his own untimely demise is both unfair and uncalled for. He is not the one on trial here and doesn't deserve to be treated so brutally by the press, even posthumously.

The high mortality rate for the infants he

delivered likely had nothing to do with his obstetric expertise but rather dumb luck. Should he be punished for taking on more difficult cases? For all we know, the unusual rates could have been due to an administrative error rather than a medical one. I'd thank you to show more care when speaking of the deceased—especially a victim.

Regards,
  Eleanor Barton

Chapter Sixteen

SARAH READ the archived letter a second time and then a third, hardly able to believe her eyes. It was all starting to come into focus. *At last.*

"She knew Dr. Karda and publicly defended him," she recapped, wondering if Finch was leaning toward the same conclusion. "Why?"

Her partner shook his head. "I don't know. Do you think maybe *she* had something to do with all the dead babies and didn't want him to take the fall for it?"

"Or they could've been working together. She told us your grandmother was stolen from the hospital. Do you think…?" She let the question trail away, believing and not believing at the same time.

"Do I think that the deaths were covers for a series of kidnappings?" He cocked his head to the side, considering. "Possibly," he added at last.

"But we only know for sure she took one baby," Sarah insisted. Eleanor was a rude and angry woman, but could she have really done something this unimaginable?

"Not Eleanor," Finch pointed out. "Eleanor didn't take my grandma. At least that's what she said. My great-grandma did. That was her sister."

"Do you think she took more babies?" Sarah asked with a tremble. Those poor mothers. Everything about this situation made her stomach twist into terrible knots. It all happened so long ago, and yet...

Finch sighed, sitting back in his chair with closed eyes as he were now picturing the scene unfold before him. "I don't know," he answered at last. "Only one person knows the answer to that."

"Are you going to go see her?" Sarah had wanted so badly to solve this mystery, and now that the pieces were starting to click together, she wanted nothing more than to take it all back. To let this horrible thing die with Eleanor.

"I don't think we have a choice," Finch said,

seeming far less upset than she did in that moment. "Perhaps if we confront her with this, she'll finally speak." He leaned toward the computer again and clicked on the print icon for the letter. "Do you know where this comes out?"

"Yeah, just a sec." Sarah stalked over to the printer and waited until their letter popped out before returning to Finch, who'd stayed behind to log off both computers. "Here you go," she said, handing it to him.

Finch folded it over twice and shoved it in his pocket. "Thanks. Are you ready for this? This could be it, you know. The big resolution to our case." His smile unnerved her. How could he not be torn in two? This was his family's past, his story.

And now her one-thing-at-a-time rule would be put to the test. If this was truly the end of their investigation into Eleanor's big secret, then that meant the next mystery they'd have to solve would be what they meant to each other.

Was she ready for that? Was he?

"I'm not coming to the hospital," she told him. "You'll have to confront her yourself."

"But why not? You are just as much as part of this as I am. Maybe more, since accessing the archives here was your idea."

Sarah shook her head, her words shaking on their way out. "She doesn't want to see me, Finch. You've got a better shot at getting to the truth than I do. Plus, I don't even know *if* I'm allowed in. I'm not family, but you are."

Finch surprised her by grabbing her hand and kissing the tops of her fingers. "Will you wait for me?"

"Wait for what? Outside the hospital? I mean, I guess, but…"

"Sure, let's start with that." His superhero smile flashed across his face, and for a moment she let herself believe that he could save her, that she wouldn't have to discover any of these answers for herself.

"But why? You don't need me to—"

He grabbed her hand again, kissed it again. "Yes, I do. Don't ever doubt that I need you. Because, one, I want you to know what happens at the first possible second. Two, I may need backup. And three, whether or not we get anything out of her today, I'm taking you out to dinner to celebrate."

Sarah wished that time could stand still—that they could stay here with the thrill of what they'd learned, together yet still apart, not needing to confront the difficult choices that lay ahead. Time, however, marched on, and so would she.

"But the case isn't solved yet," Sarah argued. "We still don't know what the rest of the numbers mean. The list."

"Then I better get it out of her, huh?" Finch let go of her hand and offered her a reassuring nod. "If that's what it takes, then that's what I'll do. I'll get the answers, Sarah. For both of us."

***

FINCH DARTED through the halls of the hospital, a homing missile zeroing in on its target more than ready for the explosion that would inevitably follow. Never had he been so eager to see his miserly aunt than in this very moment. Did they finally have enough to force a confession from her, or were there still twists and turns in this case that he couldn't even begin to fathom?

Predictably, Eleanor turned away when he entered the room. "Leave me be," she said in a strained whisper. The dark circles beneath her eyes had grown even more prominent. As much as they didn't get along, he hated to see her like this, to know she was so near her end.

"We've finally done it," he said, coming deeper into the room, needing to see the look on her face as he made his big revelation. "We figured out your mystery."

"Oh?" Eleanor looked unimpressed as she arranged the thin hospital blanket on her lap. "Well, c'mon then, let's hear it."

She doesn't believe me. She didn't think I could do it, but she wasn't counting on Sarah adding herself to the equation.

Facing the old woman now, he wanted more than anything to impress her with his knowledge, for her to know once and for all that she'd been found out, that her crimes would not be laid to rest beside her in the casket.

"The babies weren't stillborn," he said, standing at the end of her bed and waiting, waiting, waiting for her to look at him. "They were stolen. Just like my grandma. But they were reported as dead. You said your sister took her, but you were involved somehow, too."

The words tumbled out quickly, unable to be contained for even a fraction of a second longer than needed. "We found your letter to the editor. You defended him because you knew it wasn't all his fault. You were working together—the three of you and maybe more."

Eleanor finally brought her gaze to meet his. "Close, but not quite there." She smiled then. It was the first time Finch had ever seen such an expression cross her face, and it terrified him. Happy? Why now? Was it that she was finally free from carrying the guilt alone? Or had he fallen into something far more sinister than he'd once feared?

"Dr. Karda—may he rest—never had anything to do with it," Eleanor continued, her voice soft, almost pleasant. "He was as innocent as the babies we stole right out from under his nose."

It still didn't make sense. He needed to understand, needed her to tell him. "But why?" he asked, finally seeing that she may have once been a kind and good person before guilt twisted her into something unrecognizable.

"Because it was easy at the time, and very needed," Eleanor explained with another wistful smile. Everything about her had softened. Finally, she was free. He'd done this for her, along with Sarah. He hadn't wanted to help, but she'd made sure he did. And that felt like an incredible way to say both hello and goodnight to the aunt he'd never really had a chance to know.

"The baby boom that followed the war really shone a light on the couples who couldn't conceive," Eleanor said, keeping her eyes on him as she spoke. "It wasn't talked about back then like it is now. They desperately wanted children and would pay very handsomely to get them."

Finch's face crumpled into a frown, and Eleanor's followed suit. The nobleness of his effort felt tainted now. This had all been for money? All this only to save her from the guilt of her own greed?

"Don't look at me like that," she whispered, turning away. "We always chose our marks carefully. The couples paying us, they had posh lifestyles. They could afford to give the babies everything. We took them from the families who had next to nothing. It was a charity, really, giving those children a better life than they otherwise would have had."

"How could you possibly say that? You literally stole from the poor. You say they had nothing, and then you took what was left?" And he'd helped. He'd helped to absolve the crimes of a monster. Had he known…

I still would have gone through with it, he realized. To make Sarah happy, to spend time with her.

Eleanor's eyes became unfocused as she stared vacantly into the corner of the room. Finch wondered if she was seeing the past unfold again before her. Instead of answering any of his questions, she continued with her tale.

"We only took one more after the doctor's death. It became too risky after that, so we stopped. My sister wanted to keep going, but I refused. Said we'd done enough damage." Back and forth she went, one minute appearing as the benevolent savior of these lost babies and in the next, the cruel puppet master who'd pulled one too many strings.

Finch couldn't judge the past, but he desperately wanted to know how Eleanor interpreted her own role in all these events. "But you said you were doing those babies a favor, giving them a better life. Now you say you did damage. Which was it?"

A shiver ran through her, leaving the old woman wilted as it left. They'd figured this out just in time. Maybe Eleanor had been holding on for the sole purpose of passing on her tale.

"*Neither*," she said in answer to his question, and then, "*Both*. It's impossible to say. I had to believe we were helping. It was the only way to keep the guilt from suffocating me."

The pieces still weren't lining up. "So why confess now?"

"I've had a lot of time to think, sitting here waiting to die. I remember your grandma's reaction to finding out the truth, and she only ever knew a small part of it. I followed you on the news. I saw what a failure you'd become, and I wondered how different your life might have turned out if we'd never taken her."

She did this for me? It made no sense. She never even knew him before now, yet she'd voluntarily faced the weight of her crimes to help him? He still didn't understand. One very big part of the puzzle remained out of reach.

"What does the list you gave Sarah mean?" he asked. "We saw that part of one of the numbers matched up to the date of the editorial, but we can't figure out the rest." Finch shoved his phone at her, the picture of Eleanor's list enlarged on the screen.

She studied it, shaking her head. A tear rolled down her smooth cheek and plopped onto the shiny surface below. "I hardly remember myself. I kept those records so long ago. Markers of what was in the room where the baby was born, dates, info about the birth parents and the adoptive parents. So that we could find them again if ever we needed to."

"How can I find my missing family?" he said, taking the phone back, knowing the conversation had come to its end.

"I don't know, but now that you know they're out there, perhaps you can figure it out. And, Finch…" She smiled sweetly, the smile of someone who had loved and lost and perhaps found again. "I really hope you do."

Chapter Seventeen

SARAH WAITED outside the hospital as promised, although she really didn't see the point. Finch stayed inside for so long that she began to wish she had at least tried to see Eleanor with him. To pass the time, she walked several laps around the complex. When Finch still hadn't returned, she pulled out her phone and installed the Reel Life app once again.

And as she browsed through all the pictures and videos she had missed in her brief absence, she knew she'd made the right choice by rejoining. Reel Life was something Finch didn't like, but now that she'd had a bit of a break, she realized it was something she *did*. She realized now that she needed to make decisions because they were right for *her*, not because they were what someone else wanted.

Living vicariously through others meant she never really got to live at all. Her time off work had made that abundantly clear. At first she'd been lost without the patients to fill her day. Heck, she was still lost. But at least now she knew to look for a compass.

The car beeped, drawing her from her self-exploration. Finch plopped into the driver's seat and ran both hands through his hair before turning to Sarah and shaking his head. "She confessed," he said in a way that suggested he still couldn't believe it.

He caught her up on the kidnappings, the money, the written list, all of it. Finch seemed so sad in the wake of these momentous discoveries, and Sarah longed to help him feel better. To save him.

"Wow," she said when he'd finally finished. "She played God with so many lives. Including yours. How do you feel?"

"I'm really not sure. I still have to finish decoding the numbers from her list, and then I guess I'm going to find my family." He grabbed her hand and laced his fingers through hers—and she let him. The physical connection seemed to help him find his strength again. "Find as many of the families as I can."

She nodded thoughtfully. "That makes sense."

Finch sighed and pulled Sarah into a hug. The center console between them made it awkward, but he didn't seem to mind. "Thank for you doing this with me, Sarah. I would never have known without you."

Oh no. I'm doing it again. Doing what I think other people want, not figuring out what I need. Maybe one day she would end up as Mrs. Finch Jameson, but she wasn't ready to take that leap today. She needed time to think, to discover…

"You're a smart guy," she said, going limp in his arms. "You would have figured things out eventually."

"It's not just that." Finch moved one hand to Sarah's face and rubbed the apple of her cheek with this thumb. "I love that this happened now. That this horrible thing brought such a beautiful person into my life. Sarah, I'm crazy about you. Everything about my past is this messy chaos, but the future seems to clear. Looking at you."

"Finch, I…"

"Don't say anything. Not yet."

The bottoms of his eyes clenched up into a

smile. Their breaths synchronized as she waited for whatever this gorgeous man planned to tell her next. *I want him, but I don't know if I'm ready...*

"That day," he said at last. "At the zip line. I should have kissed you. I wanted to kiss you, but—"

"But?" Sarah's pulse took off at a gallop. Finch was a good man. They could be so good together, if only she could cast all her doubts aside.

Finch cupped her other cheek in his palm and moved so close that his lips brushed hers as he spoke. "I wanted our first kiss to be perfect. But now this whole mess with Eleanor, it's taught me that things won't ever be perfect. And, well--"

He crushed his lips to hers in the world's most perfect kiss. Yes, perfect did exist despite what he'd just said. A million thoughts flooded her mind as his mouth explored hers. That you could crave and fear something at the same time, that you could know and not know, that you could never really turn your thoughts off—and perhaps you shouldn't.

She'd finally gotten what she'd craved for so long...

And now she felt more confused than ever.

AFTER A BIT OF PATIENT COAXING, Finch drove with Sarah to Dorma Valley Wine that evening. It was a little out of the way vineyard he'd discovered years ago and knew it would be the perfect place for their first official date.

The proprietress showed them to a small bistro table that sat beneath an overhanging trellis. Gossamer fabric and tiny fairy lights brought the stars closer to the earth as they sipped at their wine and enjoyed matching plates of tortellini. Now that Finch had finally kissed Sarah, he found it difficult to stop and kept rising from his chair to steal little kisses between bites.

"Let me eat," Sarah said with a laugh, accepting his kiss anyway.

"I just can't believe how lucky I am," he said, and it was true. He'd undergo a million public humiliations if they all led him right here—to this night, with this woman.

She rolled her eyes playfully, but her words came out serious. "I'm nothing special."

Finch rushed to her side and kissed her again. "How could you say that? You are the most incredible, kind, and giving person I've ever met."

She set her fork down and shivered before

looking him in the eye and saying, "That's because, like Eleanor, I have a guilty conscience."

"I don't understand." He felt her pulling away from him both physically and emotionally, desperately wishing he could turn the clock back, give her more time, fix whatever had hurt her.

"She may have stolen all those babies, but I…" Sarah choked back a sob. "I killed someone."

He fell back on his haunches, just barely catching himself with his palms as he shook his head vehemently. "No, that's impossible." He refused to believe this about the woman he was falling in love with, about a woman as gentle and kind as Sarah.

Her eyelids drooped as she spoke, a shield keeping the emotions in and Finch out. "I was twelve, and it was my grandmother. I wasn't watching her like I should have, and—"

Finch found his footing again and grabbed onto both of her shoulders, forcing her to see him, to see the love and acceptance in his eyes. "Stop right there. You were a child. There's no way what happened was your fault."

She shook him off and hugged her arms around herself, and it was in that moment he knew he'd already lost her. "You can say that all you want, but it won't make it true."

He refused to give up without first giving it everything he had to offer. This wasn't just about a relationship between them. This was about Sarah's relationship with the past—her relationship with herself. She hurt so deeply, and Finch desperately wanted to fix everything for her. "So you dedicated your life to helping the elderly in your grandmother's honor. That's noble and a great tribute to her."

"No, not to remember. To forget and hope for forgiveness."

"But you've given so much to so many. It's shaped you into this incredible person who helps others."

"I'm not a person," she insisted, clenching her eyes shut again. "I'm a shell."

He pressed his lips to hers, but this time she didn't respond. "Where is this all coming from?"

She shivered as a chill rippled through the night air, and he wanted to hold her so badly—but every time he reached for her, he felt her moving farther and farther away.

"The thing with Eleanor," she said at last. "It's made me realize some things about myself."

"Stop. You are nothing like her. We all make mistakes. Accidents happen. Life goes on."

"I wish that were true," she whispered, picking up her fork again and attempting to eat.

Finch returned to his own chair to give her the space she so clearly craved, but he refused to ignore this. He would not let her shoulder these burdens on her own. He was here now. He could help make things better. If only she'd let him…

"Even if your grandmother's death was your fault, and I still don't believe it was, that one thing doesn't define you," he insisted, wishing she would look at him, wishing she would smile. "You're so much more than one thing that happened in the past."

She shrugged and continued eating. "Just like you're so much more than Reel Life?"

That one hurt, especially because Finch knew what she was saying was true. Just like her, he'd let his past define him. But unlike her, he hadn't used it to try to become a better person. He took a deep breath to make sure he had enough strength to say all that needed to be said.

"I never meant to become this social media mogul. I was just a guy that loved photography. One day I had an idea, and before I knew it, it had become this huge thing. I never wanted it, so I sold. And I felt pretty good about that decision until the entire world began to mock me. Seriously, my Google alerts were going crazy. They called me every insult under the sun. All the friends I had made left, and I ended up alone without the work I had poured myself into for so many years and without the passion that had inspired it in the first place. I made bad investments, lost a lot of money. The insults became crueler, but I never wanted all that money to begin with. I never wanted any of it. Until it was gone. Until I saw the alternative."

Sarah continued to move her pasta around the plate, not looking at him as he spoke, but at least she was listening.

Finch continued, hoping the passion came through in his words, hoping she'd understand. "Now, though, all I want is you, Sarah. I don't know who I am or what I'm going to do with the rest of my life. All I know is that I want to live it beside you. I come alive in your company. I finally feel like maybe there's something more out there that I have yet to discover. You do that for me, Sarah."

She drained the rest of her wine, then stood and offered Finch both of her hands. Together they danced under the trellis as the sun set on the horizon. As he held her close, he realized he had never been happier, never felt more like himself. She belonged in his arms just like this, pressed to his chest, their hearts beating in time. They swayed quietly for what felt like an eternity, but it also wasn't nearly long enough.

When at last they parted, Sarah had tears running down her face.

Chapter Eighteen

WITH EVERY WORD FINCH SPOKE, it became clearer and clearer to Sarah that this would be their last night together. He just didn't get it. He wanted to, but two broken parts could never make a whole. Sarah had a lot of healing to do... but so did Finch.

Wordlessly, she pulled him into a dance. Clinging to him, she pretended that they could go on like this forever. Dances often marked the beginning of something new, but in this case, it would be their goodbye.

Despite her best attempts to hold them back, the tears broke through, officially bringing an end to their one night as a couple, their one night maybe in love.

"Hey, hey... Don't cry," Finch murmured,

concern reflecting in his blue eyes. Any other day she could get lost in those eyes, lost in the smile that so often accompanied them.

But tonight she'd seen the truth, the way things needed to be.

"Finch, I really like you so much," she said, her voice quavering with each word. "But right now I don't like *me*."

Finch pulled her tight to his chest and continued to sway. "I like you enough for the both of us," he insisted after kissing the part in her hair.

Sarah's voice came out muffled against the cotton fabric of his shirt, but she hoped the meaning behind her words would be clear. "That's what I'm afraid of. Neither of us has life figured out for ourselves."

Finch stopped dancing and pulled her face up gently to meet his own. "We can figure it out together," he whispered, coming in close for a kiss but then pulling back again at the last second.

She completed the kiss. *To remember him by*, she told herself, knowing that she wasn't being fair to either of them.

"No," she said around a sob. "I need time for me, and you need time for you."

Finch laughed nervously. "That's the oldest breakup line in the book."

"Maybe so, but it's the truth. Finch, I was so busy falling in love with you that I didn't even see that I was also falling apart."

"Stop, go back to that part where you said you're falling in love with me, because—"

"No, don't. It won't make any of this easier. I wish things could have been different, but our timing's all off." She reluctantly let her arms fall away from Finch and come to rest at her sides. It was over.

Finch followed her as she walked back to the table to grab her purse. "I know things with Eleanor were—"

"This isn't about her. It's about us—me and you. Eleanor shone a light on so many things for me. I don't want to lay dying with regret and anger. I want to fix what needs fixed now. Please give me the space to do that."

He took a step back as if she'd hit him. His face became blank as if feeling anything in this moment would be far too much. "There really is no changing your mind, is there?"

"I'm sorry," she said, wrapping him in one last hug. "I'm so, so sorry."

"I think I understand," he said at last. Finch rested his chin on the top of her head as he spoke. "If our timing is off, I'll wait. One day it will be right, and I'll be ready."

"I hope you're right," she said, pressing her face into the soft fabric of his shirt to stifle her tears. "I really hope you're right."

AFTER RETURNING Sarah to her car in the college parking lot, Finch drove himself to the Cliff Walk for a midnight stroll. The trails were all but deserted at this time of night, and somehow having the space to himself served as a comfort.

I may as well get used to being on my own.

He thought he'd already grown used to being alone, but losing Sarah cut deeper than all the former business partners and fair-weather friends combined. He just couldn't accept that they were over. That's why he had come here to think.

Some way, somehow, he'd find a way to get her back.

As he searched for answers, his mind kept taking him back to their brief time together—so infatuated with both the mystery and with each other. They'd met at Cliff Walk for a new perspective, and thanks to Sarah's breeder friend, they'd found one. Carol had made it abundantly clear that she was rooting for the two of them, but what good would that do if Sarah wasn't ready to accept his love?

She'd told him from the beginning that Lucky needed to go wherever she went, and until today, the dog had been a constant third whenever they came together. Today, though, she'd arrived without her faithful companion, and today she'd also let all her insecurities tumble out and bury their fledgling relationship.

That night, she'd said a relationship between them would keep her from fixing the things inside of her that needed to be fixed, but until today, she'd used her dog in the same way—as a furry, yellow security blanket.

She'd told him that she admired him for taking his passion and turning it into something the whole world could enjoy. She didn't judge his failings but was completely unable to escape her own perceived mistakes.

How can I show her that she's already perfect?

That she's already enough all on her own?

To think she blamed herself for an accident that

happened so many years ago, that she'd been punishing herself all this time. How could he save her from her past if she was unwilling to give him any part of her future?

Sarah wanted time alone to work on herself, to heal, but she also said that he needed time for himself. Finch didn't want it, though. He only wanted her...

Wait... Is that the problem?

Does she need me to be something more, and if so, what?

A splash below drew his attention to the water. With the sky too dark to discern the shapes on the ocean, Finch pulled out his phone and activated the flashlight.

Not a pod of whales, as he'd expected, but rather a lone dinghy cutting through the gentle waves. He pictured a young couple on board that boat sharing a kiss beneath the stars. The thought made him smile—that love could still exist some-where in the world, that love carried on even when the rest of the world grew dark.

Suddenly, thankfully, *miraculously*, he knew exactly what he needed to do. It would take time, but that was exactly what Sarah had asked him for.

Chapter Nineteen

THE DAYS PASSED, and soon Sarah reached the end of her vacation time.

Unfortunately, she still hadn't figured out what she wanted from life—and why the one thing she knew she *did want* was the only one she'd tossed aside.

The sad look on Finch's face when they'd said goodbye haunted her still. Lucky also seemed to be depressed these days. No matter how much she took him to the dog park, he obviously knew something important was missing from their days. She hoped he'd be okay once they were back at work but somehow doubted that would be the case.

Ever the gentleman, Finch had respected her wishes not to call or try to see her. A part of her wished he hadn't, especially as the days wore on and brought no answers with them.

Now, like Eleanor, the only thing left for Sarah was to set things right.

She started by booking an appointment with a therapist but couldn't be seen for another few weeks. Next, she called her mother and planned a trip to visit her grandmother's grave back in Ohio. It would be the first time she'd trod ground in her hometown for over three years. High time to face the demons she'd left there.

Carol had become a constant companion these days, and together they went to visit Lucky's various siblings scattered all across the state. Sarah especially liked spending time with Grace who owned Sweets and Treats in town and now wondered why she hadn't been more receptive to the other woman's attempts at friendship in the past.

Maybe it was because all she had shone a light on all that Sarah didn't. And it wasn't just Grace. *Everyone's* life seemed so much more put together than her own. How had she never noticed it before?

How had playing by the rules gotten her so far off track?

And why did it take falling for Finch to finally realize all this?

She missed him and missed him dearly, but until she figured out who she truly wanted to be, she would never be good enough for him. She would only prolong her problems and lose him in the end.

Better to have ended it when I did she reminded herself over and over again, but this mantra offered little comfort.

Mrs. Cheung welcomed Sarah back to the rest home with a bouquet of flowers and a warm smile. "We've missed you around here," she said. "So glad to have you back again."

Everyone on staff wanted to know how she'd spent her "vacation" and whether she'd be pressing charges against Eleanor Barton for the false claim of abuse. Sarah simply answered with "not much" and "I don't know."

When the fact of the matter was she *did* know. She felt too indebted to Eleanor to press any charges. It had never been the old woman's intention to hurt her, even if her methods seemed to imply otherwise. In the end, Eleanor was just a lost soul looking for a place to belong in her final days, looking for a way to ensure she would truly rest in peace instead of tossing and turning with guilt for all of eternity.

She'd shown Sarah where she was headed with

her life if she stubbornly refused to change course —and Sarah vowed to learn from Eleanor's mistakes. She vowed to live her life differently going forward as a tribute to both her grandmother and the bitter old woman who'd unwittingly given her so much.

As Sarah began her rounds with the patients, she noticed a couple of names had been removed from her roster—people who had died without her being able to say goodbye. She read through her list again and again, saying a silent prayer for each of the departed. It struck her then that she had made a life full of constant deaths when her grandmother's death was the one thing she'd always wished she could change. She intentionally chose a profession that would rub her guilt in her face every single day of her life. Why? Did she really hate herself that much?

She took a deep breath and headed into the first patient room. It belonged to Agatha.

"Well, there you are," the old woman said, struggling to rise from her chair so she could give Sarah a big hug.

Lucky licked the old woman's fingers, causing her to laugh.

"We've missed both of you around here,"

Agatha said with another chuckle. "I'm so happy you've come back."

"Why wouldn't we come back?" Sarah asked. She was supposed to check the old woman's vitals and follow up on her medication schedule, but instead she took a seat in Agatha's vacated chair.

Agatha waved a hand dismissively. "Oh, forget I said anything."

"No, really," Sarah insisted, bracing herself for whatever revelation came back. That was the thing about working with the elderly. They had many of their own bittersweet stories to share, but they also saw into others' life with the kind of clarity that could only come from age. "Why wouldn't we come back?"

"You just seemed so…" The old woman let her words trail away, but Sarah had to know what sentiment remain hidden.

"Please," she begged. "Please tell me."

"If you insist…" Agatha sighed, leaning heavily on her cane as she regarded Sarah. "You always seemed as if you were stuck. When you went missing for a few weeks, I thought you'd figured out a way forward. But I can see now I was wrong to assume you were anywhere other than exactly where you wanted to be."

"No," Sarah said, rising back to her feet. "You're absolutely right."

"It isn't meant as an insult, dear. You see, I'm stuck, too. The difference is I want to be, and I'm not so sure you do."

Stuck. Why hadn't Sarah thought of it like that before? Nothing was missing from her life, not really. She just hadn't moved forward in so many years. She remained anchored to her grandmother's memory, anchored to her residents' past adventures, anchored to who she thought she should be. There was no way to move forward while struggling against a weight like that.

It had nothing to do with Finch or Eleanor or Lucky, and everything to do with Sarah. *She* needed to release the anchor and be brave enough to swim.

It was up to Sarah to save herself.

"Thank you so much, Agatha." She gave the old woman a tight hug. "Thank you so, so much for being honest with me. You have no idea how much you've helped."

"Oh, that's fine, dear," Agatha said, giving Sarah a dry kiss on her cheek. "I'm just happy I can still be useful to someone."

"I'll be back to see you," Sarah promised, moving toward the door. "I promise I'll be back, but first there's something important I need to do. C'mon, Lucky."

FINCH RECEIVED a call so early in the morning that the night sky still clung to the world in a dark, stifling curtain of velvet. As soon as the confusion from being awoken so suddenly wore off, he realized something terrible must have happened.

"Hello?" he mumbled into the receiver.

"It's me," an elderly woman with a voice he'd never be able to forget said. Eleanor! *Thank God she's okay!*

His great-aunt continued to force out each word with great strain. "Would you…" She stopped and took a series of deep, gasping breaths. "Would you please come see me at the hospital?"

"I'll be there in five minutes," Finch shouted, already shoving his legs into a pair of discarded jeans from the day before.

"Sorry, boy," he told his new pet Corgi named Waddles as he rushed out of the apartment. "I'll be back to walk you as soon as I can."

A month had passed since that night at the vineyard with Sarah, and in that time, Finch had begun to rebuild his life. This time on a much stronger foundation. It had started with moving out of the inn and getting his own place. Next he'd adopted Waddles, a little runt puppy with a cleft palate. No one else seemed to want him despite the breed's massive popularity—but Finch thought he was just perfect. After all, he had damage, too.

And although Waddles was still a puppy, they'd already begun the prerequisite work for his therapy dog certification. Sarah and Lucky had inspired him to add more good to the world rather than simply continuing to hide from it.

He began to form a routine that included visiting Eleanor at the hospital several times per week, catching up on all the memories they'd missed sharing, relishing in the fact that he at last had a family. The old woman had softened considerably after her confession was made, and she even sat with him on multiple occasions trying to decode the list she'd penned so long ago.

"It's funny," she'd confided in him. "My mind has let go of so many things I wish I could remember, but the one thing I actually hoped to forget hasn't left me for even a second."

When he charged into her room now, he found her lying flat on her back with her eyes closed.

Hospital equipment beeped all around her, but otherwise she was alone in a room that suddenly felt far too big for such a tiny, withered body.

"Aunt Eleanor?" he asked into the fading darkness. "I'm going to go get a doctor."

"No. Don't," she said without moving, her voice ringing like a bell. "Come here first."

He obediently brought a chair to her bedside and reached to hold one of her hands in his.

"This is it, my boy. I can't hold on any longer."

"Please just let me get the doctor. I'm sure you'll be fine if—"

Eleanor squeezed his hand to stop him. "Enough. Just listen now."

Tears stung at the corners of Finch's eyes. How was it this woman had gone from stranger to enemy to friend in such a short while?

"There's one last thing I need you to know, to set right…" She gasped for air, each breath rasping against her cracked lips, each breath a drawn-out battle.

Finch waited. She had so little strength left, and he didn't want her to use it fighting with him. He needed to hear whatever it was she had to say. For the both of them.

"Dr. Karda," Eleanor continued. "He… He

found out what we were doing with the babies, and… My sister. Lotte. She killed him for it."

Finally the last piece clicked into place. Eleanor had risked being found out to defend the doctor because she knew the truth. But she also loved her sister and couldn't betray her, no matter how wrong the other woman had been in her actions.

"I didn't find out until after, and I gave her a piece of my mind for it, too. She said she was worried they'd take your grandmother away… So, however wrong her actions—"

"She did it for love," Finch finished, hating that he could so easily understand the actions of a monster.

Eleanor coughed before continuing. "I moved out that very day. She tried to get in touch, but I couldn't forgive her for what she'd done. For me, it was enough that I keep her secret."

"All these years," Finch mumbled, shaking his head in dismay. No wonder Eleanor's anger had consumed her. She'd lost everything because of her sister's crimes. She'd had to harbor a terrible secret for more than five decades.

"All these years. I wanted you to find out for yourself, but Lotte, she did a good job covering her tracks, and so now I'm telling you what happened so that you can…" Eleanor paused and squeezed his hand again. "Find his family, tell them everything. Tell them he was a good man and a good doctor. Save his reputation. He deserves it after all these years. Let the world know."

"I will, Aunt Eleanor," he said, crying in earnest now.

"And then stop fixing the mistakes I've made with my life, and start living your own. Do it better than I did, Finch. *That's* my dying wish."

Finch sat with his great-aunt for the rest of the night, holding her hand, listening to her final stories and words of advice. Eventually the doctor did come, but by then she was gone.

Finally at peace.

Now it was up to Finch to honor her memory by finally making some good ones of his own. He was almost ready to find Sarah again, almost ready to attempt one last chance at forever with the only woman he wanted to devote his life to.

He prayed his aunt would be watching from above and that she'd be proud of the man he had yet to become.

Chapter Twenty

THE MONTHS PASSED MORE QUICKLY than Sarah had anticipated. Summer soon gave way to autumn and the small town of Redwood Cove was taken back by its locals as the tourists dispersed back to their own homes.

Sarah had considered moving back to her hometown in Ohio as well but ultimately decided against it. She'd come to the Gold Coast to build her future, and that's exactly what she intended to do. Despite the fear and guilt that had propelled her, there was still much she enjoyed about her life. She had gotten many things *almost* right.

For starters, she loved being a nurse. She'd chosen geriatrics to make amends for her grandmother's death, but found it too easy to hide in that guilt, to disappear into her patients' memories rather than making any of her own.

The past couldn't be changed. Sarah couldn't go back and undo that fateful day with her grandmother. But she could still shape the future. Her time with Finch had taught her much about herself, for which she would always owe him a debt.

Despite the heinous rule-breaking they'd engaged in at the San Francisco hospital and the lack of intel they'd gained about their mystery, Sarah had learned something very important about herself that day.

She owed that revelation to Finch, but also to a little girl named Sara without an *H*. It didn't take Sarah long to realize she wanted to work with children moving forward and that one day in the far-off, distant future she wanted to have children of her own, too.

She thought about it a lot now—*the future.* She'd once been too terrified to think about life more than a day at a time, but now she found herself both making plans and carrying through with them.

Like today. She'd agreed to go on some new whale-watching tour with Carol and the dogs. She'd always loved the majestic sea creatures, but they'd become even more special now that they also reminded her of her brief time with Finch.

She cherished their past but no longer allowed herself to be held back by it. Instead, she eagerly agreed to join Carol for the chance to experience something new. Besides, Lucky still loved whales, too, and he deserved a fun day out.

"I feel like I haven't seen you in forever," Carol squealed, running forward to give Sarah a tight hug before they both boarded the modest-sized tour boat and found an open spot on the deck to stand with the dogs. "How's the new job?"

"I love it," Sarah admitted with a huge smile. With a blast of its horn, the boat pulled away from the dock, and a rush of salty sea air whipped Sarah's long loose waves against her neck.

"You seem so much happier these days," Carol pointed out, slurping iced coffee through a reusable metal straw.

"I *feel* so much happier these days," Sarah admitted as she reached down to pet her Golden Retriever's head. "I think Lucky is, too."

"Good, because you really had me worried there for a bit."

Sarah laughed and looped an arm over her friend's shoulders. "No more worrying about me.

Just keep raising up the best dogs in the whole world. We need more good boys like Lucky."

Lucky's tongue lolled out the side of his mouth as he sat happily panting beside his parents.

"Now that, I can do," Carol promised with a wink. "Speaking of, we should have another reunion for all the owners and dogs soon. Will you and Lucky be there?"

"We wouldn't miss it for the world."

"Do you promise? Even if you're mad at me, you'll still come?"

"Carol, why would I be mad at you?" Sarah bit her lip in confusion. Carol had been her most constant friend since she'd relocated to California, and other than their brief argument over Sarah deleting her Reel Life account, the two had never fought.

"Well, I…" Carol's cheeks grew bright red as she shifted her weight from foot to foot. All of a sudden, she shouted, "Look, a whale!" She pointed animatedly to the ocean. Still confused, Sarah turned to follow her finger…

But, despite the name of the tour, there was no whale in sight.

And when she turned back toward her friend to demand answers, there was no Carol, either.

Even more flustered now, Sarah turned in the other direction, wondering what in the heck was going on.

And that's when at last she saw.

Not a whale, but rather Finch Jameson, walking toward her with a bouquet of yellow flowers in his arms and a smile stretched across his unforgettably handsome face.

Oh, how she had missed that face…

FINCH'S KNEES felt weak as he walked across the boat deck toward Sarah. He'd seen her when she boarded with Carol, and it took everything he had not to run to her then.

What ultimately kept him back was the fact he'd planned their grand reunion down to the second and didn't want to spoil any part of it.

"*You*," Sarah said, her bright hazel eyes widening despite the beginnings of tears that threatened to spill.

"Please let those be happy tears," he mumbled, passing the flowers to her. There was so much he needed to say, it was as if all the words were fighting to come out at once, leaving him in a bumbling mess.

She nodded and inhaled the sweet scent of the bouquet.

"Daffodils for new beginnings," he explained, gesturing to the flowers. "Figured they couldn't hurt."

"Thank you, but what are you doing here?" Sarah asked breathlessly.

He longed to take her in his arms and never let go, to tell her how these past few months without her had been torture—though a necessary one. Mostly he wanted to hear Sarah say they could start again.

Finch chuckled softly, trying not to let the momentousness of the occasion overwhelm him. "Well, you see," he said with a smile, "this is my boat."

Carol returned to Sarah's side and took the flowers from her arms. "Well, you don't *seem* mad," she said with a laugh that matched his own.

"You set me up!" Sarah said, feigning anger but failing to wear anything but a smile on her flushed face.

"It seems I did," Carol replied, patting Sarah on the shoulder before leaving them again and taking the dogs with her as she crossed to the other side of the deck.

"I needed to see you again," Finch continued as Sarah's gaze fell back to him. "To tell you *you made the right call back then.* I didn't deserve you then, but I hope with everything I've got that I do now."

"And so you bought a boat?" she asked, her voice cracking and lips smiling. How could he ever convey just how much she'd changed him for the better? How clearly she'd shown him he needed to change for himself, too? Words would never be enough, but hopefully when she learned all he'd done…

He licked his lips and placed a hand on his heart. "Well, like you said, I needed to find me again. I needed to stop hiding from my past and so, yeah, I bought a boat and started a new company. Welcome to Gold Coast Whale Tours. Doesn't have quite the same ring as Reel Life, but you know—"

Sarah threw her arms around his neck and pulled him in close. The surprise of this gesture caused Finch to fall silent.

"You did this all for me?" she murmured close to his ear.

"No," he whispered. "I did it for me. You were right all along, Sarah. I needed to get back to my passion. It was never about running some big business, being some hotshot billionaire. It was always about the art, about capturing life frame by frame."

"And you chose whales because…" Sarah let her words fall away. Was she too shocked to acknowledge the meaning behind his choice? Unwilling to take any credit for what he'd done in her honor? As it turned out his sweet Sarah would always need a little coaxing, would always be a little shy—and he loved her for that.

"Remember on Cliff Walk?" he asked, helping her along. "How time just seemed to stand still when that family of orcas swam past? Everything stopped, everyone stopped, and we just lived for that moment. I want more moments like that, Sarah. I want them for me, and I want them for us. Please tell me there can be an us."

She answered by bringing her lips to his in a kiss that was as sweet as she'd always been. When she pulled away, she wore a devastatingly gorgeous grin that was meant just for him.

"I missed you. I was always hoping we'd see each other again, but I never imagined…" She shook her head subtly and laughed through freshly flowing tears.

"That I'd get a clue?"

She laughed again and hugged him tighter "Maybe."

"Hey, I may be slow on the uptake, but luckily there's this amazing woman who taught me all I needed to know when it came to finding clues and solving mysteries."

"So you've solved the mystery of Sarah, huh?"

"No, you are the one thing that's always made sense. It was me who was the mystery all along."

"And did you solve it?"

"It's a work in progress, but if we wait for all the pieces to line up, we'll never get to appreciate the beautiful picture forming in front of us."

"Finch, that's so…" She stopped and took in a shaky breath. "That's so corny. You scripted this whole thing out, didn't you?"

He laughed at himself. "Yeah, maybe I did. But I knew I'd only get one chance to make things right, and I—"

Sarah pressed a finger to his lips. "No. There's never just one chance. Every day is a new chance, a new beginning."

"And how about today?" he asked with a slight smirk.

Before Sarah could answer, a crowd of passengers rushed to their side of the deck, whispering and pointing excitedly. Finch and Sarah turned together and watched as a pair of gray whales breeched the surface before disappearing back beneath the ocean in one beautiful, synchronized movement. Everyone stood silent waiting for the whales to surface again.

When at last they did, Sarah pressed her lips to Finch's cheek and whispered, "Today is the first day of the rest of our lives... *together*."

Epilogue

SARAH SIFTED through her closet in search of the perfect summer dress to wear for the reunion—not for the dog families, but rather for Finch's long-lost extended family. They'd been dating for close to a year now, and each day Sarah felt more and more confident that she had made the right decision by waiting.

Finch loved his work with the whale-watching tour and was even working on a book of photography set to be released by a major publisher in the coming year. Sarah, too, loved working with children, and together she and Finch put together some of the highest-earning fundraisers in the history of the Make A Wish Foundation.

Sarah had once been too afraid to make any wishes for herself, but somehow she'd still managed to catch a falling star. Finch was that star. Eleanor, too. They often visited her grave site together and even brought Lucky to pay his respects on more than one occasion.

Lucky, too, had found love. From the moment he first laid eyes on Finch's little Corgi, Waddles, the much larger Golden Retriever had been a goner. In turn, the puppy learned the therapy dog trade under Lucky's careful guidance, and now the two worked as a duo with Sarah on days they got to visit the children at the hospital. Other days they rode on Finch's sight-seeing boat, never growing tired of the whales and dolphins that came over to say hello.

Once Sarah and Finch were together again they'd worked tirelessly toward cracking the coded clues in Eleanor's list. And, sure enough, once they'd figured out that the numbers included partial social security numbers and a mix of local zip codes, they'd been able to begin locating the stolen babies.

Of course, many of the babies were now retirees themselves, having lived their entire lives not knowing anything was amiss. Some refused to believe the news, but others committed themselves to finding their missing kin.

And Finch insisted on funding every single search himself.

Even if they'd never been related by blood, it was his great-aunt and great-grandmother who had caused this mess in the first place—and as part of repenting for their sins, he wanted to ensure he "set things right" just as Eleanor had requested from the beginning.

Today he'd at last be meeting his own missing family, and Sarah would be by his side the entire time. The best part was that they had used Reel Life to seek out his relatives, meaning his biggest failure also became the impetus for his biggest success.

Finch and Sarah would be meeting with forty-odd relations at the Dorma Valley vineyard that day. Sarah questioned why he'd want to start a new chapter in his life where they had ended their own incomplete love story just over a year ago, but he'd just shrugged and said it was one of the only places with enough space for everyone.

Settling at last on a bright yellow, retro-inspired A-line party dress and navy blue flats, Sarah pulled her hair into a bun and rushed outside to meet

Finch whose car idled in her driveway. Even though he knew she always needed extra time to get ready, he never failed to show up at least five minutes early.

Some things never changed, and for that, she was quite thankful.

"Hi, honey," she said, leaning through the open window to kiss Finch on the cheek before settling Lucky in the back with Waddles.

"Are you ready for today?" she asked as she took her seat and buckled in.

Finch took a deep breath. His hands shook on the wheel as he reversed out of her driveway. "As I'll ever be," he answered.

They chatted idly on their way to the vineyard, but mostly Sarah left Finch to his thoughts. This would be a huge day for him. It could change everything, but she also knew that the strong man she loved could handle whatever life hurtled his way.

Although they arrived early, the parking lot was already overflowing with a mix of SUVs, cars, and trucks sporting license plates from at least six different states.

Yes, today was going to be huge.

Finch opened her door for her and then took her hand in his, leading her gently across the gravel lot and toward the same trellised area where she'd broken both their hearts not all that long ago.

When they turned the corner, they were greeted by a roaring crowd. Everyone held a framed photo, waving them high in the air as they cheered. The dogs went crazy, running back and forth, weaving in and out of the crowd and sucking in all the delectable new smells.

"What's all this?" Sarah asked with a confused smile spreading across her face.

"Sarah, this is my family," he answered, gesturing toward the sea of smiling faces. "And, well, I was hoping you'd help me complete an otherwise perfect picture."

She breathed in a slow, shaky breath, glancing again toward the framed photos held by each found relative of Finch's. Only then did she realize that none of the photos held a complete picture on its own.

A murmur rippled through the crowd as the people began to reorganize themselves, pushing their pictures together to form one giant image. She strained as it came into focus, then gasped when she recognized Finch.

On one knee, holding…

She spun around so fast she almost lost her balance, but there was Finch kneeling before her in real life, too, with one hand on his heart and the other steadying her at the waist.

He let out a sharp whistle, and Lucky trotted over carrying a small basket with a velvet box inside. "Thank you, Lucky," he said, taking the box and holding it open before Sarah. A beautiful antique, square-cut amethyst sparkled amidst a background of white silk.

"It was my great-aunt Eleanor's," he said with one of his world-stopping smiles. "Sarah, would you—?"

"Yes!" she shouted, tears spilling down her flushed cheeks.

"Would you *let me finish?*" he said with a laugh, eliciting similar chuckles from the crowd of his family gathered close by.

She laughed, sobbed, and then nodded.

"I've searched far and wide to locate my missing family, but it's still not complete. Not without you. Sarah, will you do me the great honor of becoming my wife? I promise to love you until—"

Sarah didn't need to hear anymore. She tackled Finch to the ground and showered him with kisses.

Lucky and Waddles joined in with tails wagging and tongues licking.

And that was when Sarah knew that everything was exactly as it should be. Only one question remained…

How'd she get so lucky?

Afterword

Have you ever been loved by a dog?

Because it changes your life.

Dogs are the most faithful friends you will ever make. They love you unfailingly—even when you don't deserve it.

Perhaps especially then.

They share your life with you and only ask for a kind word, a comforting pat, a bit of your attention in return.

This book is for my own Golden Oldie, Polo.

He was my very first dog. He's the good boy that made me into a truly devoted dog lover!

I still remember when I first met him and his litter-mates nearly a decade ago. They'd only just opened their eyes and still needed more time with their mother, but even then, I knew that wrinkled little ball of  blond fluff was meant to be mine.

And especially now, when I look at that same face, whitened with age, I see a lifetime of memories made together. I know he won't be by my side for too much longer, but I'm thankful for each and every day.

 Polo is the kind of dog who will lick away your tears, and not just because the salt from them tastes yummy. He always knows when I need him.

When I was going through a high-risk pregnancy, he never left my side. He even gave up sleep in the final weeks, so he could watch over me as I slept. Any toss, any turn, he was there with his warm nose and a reassuring lick.

He was a friend when I needed one more than anything.

When my first marriage fell to shambles, he stood faithfully by my side and reminded me that I was worth loving after all—at least to him.

He watched as I fell in love again, this time for real. He knew even before I did that Mr. Storm was meant to be ours forever. When we had our little girl, he loved her, too. Through the aches and pains of arthritis and other old age ailments, he encourages her to cuddle him, to love him as best she can even if it's a little rough.

What have the last ten years been like?

They've been a life full of love, loss, heartbreak, triumph, and everything in between. They've been a life spent loving a dog. We experienced it all together, my good boy and me.

Have you ever been loved by a dog?

I pray you have, because it's one of those special parts of life that no one should miss.

I love you, Polo. Thank you for being there every step of the way. Thank you for being my good boy.

Acknowledgments

This book wouldn't have been possible without my amazing series sisters, S.B. Alexander, Ann Omasta, Becky Muth, Pauline Creeden, and Emmie Lyn—you ladies inspire me daily with your talent, passion, and commitment. Thank you for being a part of this!

To my support team, who is always there (no matter how late I am in meeting my deadline): Megan Harris, Mallory Rock, and Jasmine Bryner.

To the many other amazing authors and readers who have joined Sweet Promise Press and shared in my vision for creating a clean and wholesome publisher that produces entertaining books and lasting friendships.

To all the cool cats I partied with at the

Romance Writers of America conference in Denver when I should have been working a little (or a lot!) harder to get my book written in time.

To my friends, family, husband, daughter. Everything I do is made possible by you!

To my intrepid assistant and friend, Angi Hegner, and to the 10,088 fictional Angis that my daughter has invented in her imagination—because my one Angi *really does* somehow manage to do the work of at least 10,000 others. Yup, she is that awesome!

And to Angi's new husband, Gus, for making her happy and loving her the way she has always deserved to be loved. Congrats on your wedding, and many happy years to come!

To my family of dogs, and to the real-life canine heroes who comfort the dying and offer them a friend in their final days and hours of life.

To anyone who feels that their life isn't worth celebrating, that it isn't enough: Yes, my darlings, it is! Get out there and live the best you know how. It's never too late to make a change, and it's never too late to find the real you.

To everyone, thanks for reading and allowing me to live my dream day after day. You guys really are the best of the best!

Sneak Peek

Read the first chapter of RESCUING RILEY, book 2 of the Gold Coast Retrievers...

Riley Lewis walked out of the Sacramento airport and into an oven. The temperature had to be a hundred degrees or more, and even though she didn't feel an ounce of humidity like she usually did in Boston, she felt as though she were suffocating.

On the flip side, Riley also felt free for the first time in over a month. She'd shut herself off from the rest of the world to brood over a breakup that had hit her right between the eyes. She was madder at herself than she was at the jerk she'd thought wanted a serious relationship—mad because she hadn't seen the forest for the trees. She was usually in tune to the signs. After all, her dad had cheated on her mom. But Riley had been so preoccupied with her job as a wedding planner that she hadn't been focused on her relationship.

Regardless, Riley and her ex, John had never exchanged the word "love." They'd never expressed their feelings to one another. She couldn't say she loved him. Her best friend Liza had said her ego was shattered. Maybe so. But Riley did like John a lot. He had a big heart. He had a great job as a sales rep for a technology company, and he'd treated her well.

Outside Sacramento Airport, people were in a hurry, darting around others who were hugging loved ones, or dumping their suitcases into cars before they drove off.

Riley texted Liza to let her know she was standing outside baggage claim. The last time they talked, which was the night before, Liza told Riley she would be waiting in the cell phone lot.

Cars slowed to a crawl, and drivers scanned the crowd around Riley for their guests.

She waited for the ping, alerting her to a text from Liza, but there was nothing, not even the three dots that indicated someone was typing.

Suddenly, Riley got an eerie chill, as though something bad was about to happen, but she shook it off. The plane had landed a few minutes early, and she'd told Liza to give her thirty minutes after she got off the plane to get her luggage.

She navigated through the waiting passengers and found a quiet spot at the end of the glass building, near the taxicab stands to lean against. Then she sent Liza another text to let her know where she was. While Riley waited, she people-watched, which was something she loved to do. A mom scolded her five-year-old son. A businessman typed on his phone. And two lovers embraced.

She sighed. John and Riley had done that very thing when he'd returned after a week on the road. She missed feeling a man's arms around her, giving her that sense that someone cared for her in an intimate way.

But as her brother, Ross, kept telling her, "John was never going to get serious with you."

Again, she was mad at herself for not seeing the signs. Some of his actions should've clued her in. Granted, he traveled around the country for his job. Showing up late for their date or cancelling on Riley at the last minute because of a delayed or missed flight wasn't unheard of. But toward the end, his excuses had piled up until she confronted him. When she did, he caved, spilling his guts on how he was seeing another woman who lived in Chicago.

Thinking about that still stung. Liza had recommended that Riley get away from the fast pace of Boston and her job. She'd debated long and hard. As a wedding planner, Riley's job was nonstop most of the year, but busier than ever from May to September. But that August, she had only two clients getting married. Otherwise, she wouldn't have been sweating in over hundred-degree heat, although she had two awesome assistants who could handle the big day for one of her clients while she was away.

Besides, the last time Riley had seen her BFF was over a year ago when Liza was boarding a plane to move back to Northern California. Riley missed her terribly. They'd talked once a week since Liza left, but as of late, Liza had been checking on Riley since her breakup.

Their plans while Riley was there were to kick back and see the sights of NorCal, maybe tour a winery or two, and visit Redwood Cove. Liza had mentioned there was a ton to do in the quaint town, like whale watching, great sea life, and zip lining if

Riley was into that. But she wasn't one for heights. She felt that testing her fate on a thin line and flying at high speeds over some ravine or canyon was suicide. She didn't even like roller coasters. Riley had been traumatized once when she was a little girl, and since then, no one could coax her onto one; even peer pressure didn't work.

Nevertheless, Riley couldn't wait to wrap her arms around Liza. She couldn't wait to talk into the wee hours of the morning and hear all about Liza's job at a top-notch fashion company in San Francisco— Stitches Inc. Liza hardly talked about her job on the phone, although when she did, it was about some new design she was working on and a fashion show or two.

Riley couldn't be happier for Liza. When Liza had lived in Boston, she had worked for a fashion company that was eventually raided by the FBI. Her former employer was one of the prominent mafia families in Boston. Liza hadn't known that when she'd gotten hired, and she'd told the FBI that she had never seen anything illegal.

After the raid, Liza had quit and searched for another job for months. Every company she'd interviewed with had been frank with her, saying, "You worked for one of the largest mafia families in the New England area. We don't want trouble."

Liza had decided to spread her wings and look at companies around the country, concentrating on San Francisco. Most of her family lived in the NorCal area, but she wasn't exactly close to her dad. However, she was tight with her cousin Josh, who Riley hadn't met yet.

Anyway, since Riley had made the decision to come two weeks ago, the airlines didn't have many flights available to choose from among the airports in the NorCal area. So she had to settle on Sacramento and flying out on Thursday instead Friday like Riley had wanted to. Besides, Fridays were a busy day for travel. John had always complained about how airports were packed and flights were overbooked on Fridays.

A taxicab driver wearing a San Francisco Giants ball cap came up to Riley. "Do you need a ride?"

The baggage claim area was thinning out, and the sun was dipping behind the three-story parking garage across from her.

"No, thank you," she said. "I'm waiting on my ride."

He quietly went back to his cab adjacent to her.

She called Liza, and the line went straight to voice mail. *Odd*.

As long as she'd known Liza, she wasn't the type to be late. That eerie feeling Riley had gotten earlier came back with a vengeance. She didn't have a backup plan, although she could get a rental car easily. In fact, she'd suggested to Liza that she would do just that, but Liza had insisted on picking her up. "The drive will give us more time to catch up," Liza had said.

Don't panic. She's twenty minutes late. She'll show up.

Someone coughed as they walked past Riley, causing her to snap back to the present and helping her to shed some of the cold chill that seemed to be seeping into Riley's veins.

She peeked around the building for no other reason than to take a breath and tell herself nothing had happened to Liza.

Blood orange colored the horizon in the distance.

Her off-the-shoulder blouse was starting to stick to her as the sweat trickled down her back and stomach. It was time to go back into the air-conditioned building while she decided on her next move.

Once inside, the aroma of coffee hit her, and

her taste buds perked up. Suddenly, Riley's body was starting to feel the three-hour time change.

Her phone rang as she was about to get in line for some much-needed caffeine. She answered it without looking at the screen. "Liza, where are you?"

"Sis," Riley's brother, Ross, said. "You sound panicked. What's going on?"

Her twin brother knew her sometimes better than she knew myself, although it wasn't hard to detect the hitch in her voice.

Riley slid over to a quiet spot near the elevator. "I can't get ahold of Liza. She's late. Like thirty minutes late now."

"I knew I should've come with you," he said.

"I'm a big girl." She tried to fill her tone with confidence, but with the panic coursing through her, Riley was failing badly.

One of Riley's flaws was that she jumped to conclusions too quickly and immediately thought the worst. She couldn't help it, though. She had grown up in a rough neighborhood, with a cheating dad, then a single mom after her mom had kicked out my cheating dad. Plus, the Lewis house had been robbed several times. Looking over her shoulder had become the norm, especially when Ross wasn't with her.

"Besides, I'm on a girls' trip with my bestie. No men allowed."

"What are you going to do, then?" Ross asked.

"I'm going to call her office first, and if I strike out, then her cousin Josh."

"You mean the ex-Navy SEAL?" Ross asked a little excitedly.

Her brother was into military and war movies. He even loved to watch those programs on how Navy SEALs train. He'd wanted to go into the military but had decided against it when their parents had gotten a divorce. Ross hadn't wanted to leave Riley and their mom alone.

Riley's phone alerted her to an incoming call from a number she didn't recognize. "Hold on. This might be Liza now." She switched over to answer.

"Hi, Riley. I'm Taylor, Liza's assistant. She's stuck in a meeting with an important client. Is there any way you can rent a car and head to her cousin's bed and breakfast in Redwood Cove? I'll text you the address. She also said she would call as soon as she can."

It seemed Riley was renting a car after all. "I'm

supposed to stay with her at her apartment. I can meet her there."

"No. She insisted that you head to Redwood Cove Inn. It's going to be a late night for her."

A bed and breakfast sounded so much better than an apartment in the city anyway. "Okay, but have her call me as soon as she can, though."

"I will." Then the line went dead.

She switched back to Ross. "Liza got stuck at work. I'm going to rent a car and make my way to Josh's in Redwood Cove. I'll check in with you when I get there."

"You better. Or I'm taking the next flight out."

She laughed, even though he was serious. He'd always been so protective of her.

"I have my mace if that makes you feel better." Mace wouldn't completely stop an attacker, but it would slow someone down, allowing her time to get away.

"Call me as soon as you get there," he said. "Do you hear me?"

"Loud and clear." She hung up before he could give Riley his speech on "Make sure you look at what's around you. Don't forget to use the mace and knee them in the groin if you have to."

While Riley was a confident woman, she was a

little leery about finding her way to Redwood Cove. Not because of getting attacked, but because darkness would set in soon, and she wasn't a great nighttime driver.

Want to keep reading? Head to www.SweetPromisePress.com/GoldCoast to grab your copy now!

What's our Sweet Promise? It's to deliver the heart-warming, entertaining, clean, and wholesome reads you love with every single book.

From contemporary to historical romances to suspense and even cozy mysteries, all of our books are guaranteed to put a song in your heart and a smile on your face. That's our promise to you, and we can't wait to deliver upon it...

We release one new book per week, which means the flow of sweet, relatable reads coming your way never ends. Make sure to save some space on your eReader!

Check out our books in Kindle Unlimited at
sweetpromisepress.com/Unlimited

Pre-order upcoming series bundles to save at
sweetpromisepress.com/Shop

Join our reader discussion group, meet our authors,
and make new friends at
sweetpromisepress.com/Group

Sign up for our weekly newsletter at
sweetpromisepress.com/Subscribe

And don't forget to like us on Facebook at
sweetpromisepress.com/FB

Six special Golden Retrievers help their humans solve mysteries, save lives, and even find love…

SAVING SARAH BY MELISSA STORM

Sarah Campbell loves living vicariously through the residents at the Redwood Cove Rest Home. But when a surly patient insists she can't die before "setting things right," Sarah finds she may end up taking on far more than she ever bargained for… especially since all signs point to murder. Have she and her therapy dog Lucky stumbled upon the key to solving the most famous cold case in Gold Coast history?

Despite creating the world's most popular social network, Finch Jameson lives a life of ashamed solitude. The last thing he wants is to draw attention to himself, but that's exactly what happens when a distant relative delivers an earth-shattering confession in her dying days. Soon he finds himself more intrigued by the shy and beautiful nurse who's committed to helping him solve his great-aunt Eleanor's mystery than in the mystery itself. But will she ever let her guard down long enough to let him in?

Can Finch and Sarah work together to solve Eleanor's big mystery before time runs out? And might redeeming Eleanor's legacy somehow save them both in the process?

Get your copy at
SweetPromisePress.com/GoldCoast

Rescuing Riley by S.B. Alexander

Riley Lewis may plan weddings for a living, but it doesn't mean she believes in love. However, love may be just what she gets when she lays eyes on the disabled veteran running the bed and breakfast that will serve as her home during a much-needed visit with her best friend.

Joshua Bandon wanted one thing when he was discharged from the military—peace and quiet. But when his service dog, Charlie, falls hard for a beautiful woman staying at their inn, he just may end up following suit.

When Riley's best friend disappears without warning, Josh and Charlie may be the only ones who can help... Especially when Riley goes missing too.

Get your copy at
SweetPromisePress.com/GoldCoast

GUARDING GRACE BY ANN OMASTA

Grace Wilson loves the wonderful life she has created with her daughter in picturesque Redwood Cove, California—even if she is a bit lonely. To add to their family, mom and daughter adopt a sweet "Golden Wetweevuh" puppy. And they're not the only ones who think Star is, well, a star. A television show casts the pup for a role, but it's the co-host that has Grace's heart doing tricks.

Dash Diamond is a local celebrity with a megawatt smile. He is less than thrilled when his show's producers inform him that a puppy has been cast in a new role. But his new co-star comes with an owner who makes Dash see stars when he looks at her.

When Star is puppy-napped and held for ransom, all attention goes to her rescue. Grace and Dash can't act on their undeniable romantic spark of attraction while the pup is possibly in danger. Star is the missing piece. Will they find her in time to complete their puzzle?

Get your copy at ### *SweetPromisePress.com/GoldCoast*

PROTECTING PEYTON BY BECKY MUTH

Peyton McIntyre's brother is missing. Local police claim they're looking into it, but hope dwindles as the days continue to pass without any answers. Worse still, her only chance of finding him may depend on a rookie officer who sends her temper flaring and her heart quivering.

Kurt Collins is a fourth-generation police officer, but so far he hasn't been able to live up to his family's long legacy of service. When the infuriating and beautiful Peyton asks for his help, he wonders if she might hold the key to the recognition he craves. Last time they met, her dog, Gilda, saved his life. This time she just might be able save his reputation.

As they begin their search it appears that Peyton's brother may not want to be found. Unfortunately, failing to complete this assignment could risk both Kurt's career and any chance he has at winning Peyton's heart. Is a happy ending even possible, or will Peyton and Kurt both lose everything before they're through?

Get your copy at
SweetPromisePress.com/GoldCoast

Finding Felicity by P. Creeden

Despite a difficult childhood, Felicity Stilton never gave up on her dreams. Now, as an adult, she and her Golden Retriever, JJ, help special needs children pave the way for their own futures. Everything is perfect, until she gets the one call she never expected to receive.

Officer Darren Willis hates that it falls to him to tell the beautiful and inspiring Felicity her birth mother has taken her own life. Although the case appears to be open-and-shut, the grieving daughter insists something foul is afoot. Will he be brave enough to follow dark clues into the past along side the one woman with whom he just might want to make a future?

Only Darren believes Felicity's suspicions and is willing to help investigate what really happened to her long-lost mother. When the signs begin to point to murder, Darren worries Felicity might be next… But should he abandon the case to protect her even if it means losing the woman he loves forever?

***Get your copy at
SweetPromisePress.com/GoldCoast***

HELPING HANNA BY EMMIE LYN

For Hanna Moss, love has always come with danger. From the incessant stalking by an ex to nearly losing her life in a hit and run accident, she vows to remain alone--and safe. So when her golden retriever, Bella, welcomes a handsome private investigator into their lives Hanna is surprised to find herself willing to open up despite the tremendous risks that have always come with letting others in.

Blake Bowman returns to Redwood Cove with a shattered heart. All he wants is to enjoy a much-needed quiet vacation far from his ex-girlfriend. At least, that was the plan until he meets Hanna—beautiful and with an injury that is more than skin deep. He'll need to stay focused, though, because it looks like what happened to her was no accident.

Blake desperately wants to help Hanna in every way possible, even if that means putting love on hold. Hanna is terrified of the feelings she's rapidly developing for Blake and refuses to repeat her past mistakes... Is Hanna safer on her own, or will trusting Blake finally allow her to heal?

Get your copy at
SweetPromisePress.com/GoldCoast

Get Text Updates

Well, here's something cool… You can now sign up to get text notifications for all my most important book news. You can choose to receive them for New Releases, New Pre-Orders, or Special Sales--or any combination of the three.

These updates will be short, sweet, and to the point with a link to the new book or deal on your favorite retailer.

You choose when you receive them, making this new way of communicating fully customized to your needs as a reader.

Sign up at www.MelStorm.com/TextMe

More from Melissa Storm

Sign up for free stories, fun updates, and uplifting messages from Melissa at www.MelStorm.com/gift

---

The Sled Dog Series
Get ready to fall in love with a special pack of working and retired sled dogs, each of whom change their new owners' lives for the better.

Let There Be Love
Let There Be Light
Let There Be Life
Season of Mercy

Season of Majesty
Season of Mirth

The First Street Church Romances
Sweet and wholesome small town love stories with the community church at their center make for the perfect feel-good reads!

Love's Prayer
Love's Promise
Love's Prophet
Love's Vow
Love's Trial
Love's Treasure
Love's Testament
Love's Gift

The Alaska Sunrise Romances
These quick, light-hearted romances will put a smile on your face and a song in your heart. It's time to indulge in a sweet Alaskan get-away!

Must Love Music
Must Love Military
Must Love Mistletoe
Must Love Mutts
Must Love Mommy
Must Love Moo
Must Love Mustangs
Must Love Miracles
Must Love Mermaids
Must Love Movie Star

The Church Dogs of Charleston
A very special litter of Chihuahua puppies born on Christmas day is adopted by the local church and immediately set to work as tiny therapy dogs.

Little Loves
Mini Miracles
Dainty Darlings
Tiny Treasures

The Memory Ranch Romances
This new Sled Dogs-spinoff series harnesses the restorative power of both horses and love at Elizabeth Jane's therapeutic memory ranch.

Memories of Home
Memories of Heaven
Memories of Healing

The Finding Mr. Happily Ever After Series
One bride, four possible grooms, unlimited potential for disaster to strike. Is the man waiting at the end of the aisle the one that's meant to be Jazz's forever love?

Nathan
Chase
Xavier
Edwin
The Finale

Stand-Alone Novels and Novellas
Whether climbing ladders in the corporate world or taking care of things at home, every woman has a story to tell.

Angels in Our Lives
A Mother's Love
A Colorful Life

Special Collections & Boxed Sets
From light-hearted comedies to stories about finding hope in the darkest of times, these special boxed editions offer a great way to catch up or to fall in love with Melissa Storm's books for the first time.

Small Town Beginnings: A Series Starter Set
The Sled Dog Series: Books 1-5
The First Street Church Romances: Books 1-3
The Alaska Sunrise Romances: Books 1-5
Finding Mr. Happily Ever After: Books 1-5
True Love Eternal: The 1950's Collection

About the Author

Melissa Storm is a mother first, and everything else second. Writing is her way of showing her daughter just how beautiful life can be, when you pay attention to the everyday wonders that surround us. So, of course, Melissa's USA Today bestselling fiction is highly personal and often based on true stories.

Melissa loves books so much, she married fellow author Falcon Storm. Between the two of them, there are always plenty of imaginative, awe-inspiring stories to share. Melissa and Falcon also run a number of book-related businesses together, including LitRing, Sweet Promise, Press, Novel Publicity, Your Author Engine, and the Author Site. When she's not reading, writing, or child-rearing, Melissa spends time relaxing at home in the company of a seemingly endless quantity of dogs and a rescue cat named Schrödinger.

GET IN TOUCH!
www.MelStorm.com
author@melstorm.com